Also by Cecile R. Bauer

Mumma's Favorite
A Lorena McGee Mystery
Yellowback Mysteries, 2008

Justice for Daddy's Little Girl
A Lorena McGee Mystery
Yellowback Mysteries, 2011

The Monster Within:
A True Tale of Terror and Salvation
Seaboard Press, 2009

Cherish Every Moment
Seaboard Press, 2009

Stepping Stones
Meditations and Prayers for Spiritual Renewal
Paulist Press, 1999

Caregiver's Gethsemane
Practical and Spiritual Help for Caregivers to the Dying
Paulist Press, 1995

Escape to Sun City
Old Fogies on Motorcycles Rob A Bank and Head West
Northwest Publishing, 1989 / Books in Motion, 2001

Angels Get No Respect
Humorous Tales of Angels on Earth
Magnificat Press, 1987

Mona/Lu
Help and Healing for Parents with Anger Issues
Magnificat, 1987

Living, Losing and Learning
A Faith Journey from Bitter Grief to Peaceful Acceptance
Seaboard Press, 2017

Sister Susanna and the Rosary Mysteries

Sister Susanna and the Rosary Mysteries

A Lorena McGee Mystery

Cecile R. Bauer

YELLOWBACK MYSTERIES
JAMES A. ROCK & COMPANY, PUBLISHERS
FLORENCE • SOUTH CAROLINA

Sister Susanna and the Rosary Mysteries by Cecile R. Bauer

is an imprint of JAMES A. ROCK & CO., PUBLISHERS

Sister Susanna and the Rosary Mysteries
copyright ©2017 by Cecile R. Bauer

Address comments and inquiries to:

YELLOWBACK MYSTERIES
James A. Rock & Company, Publishers
1937 West Palmetto Street, #248
Florence, SC 29501

E-mail:
jarock@sprintmail.com   lar-rock@earthlink.net

Paperback ISBN: 978-1-59663-883-4

Printed in the United States of America

First Edition: 2017

Dedication

To all the selfless women who dedicate
Their lives to serving God and others
And
To all Nuns everywhere

Thank you for being our
Angels on earth

A NOTE FROM THE AUTHOR

Who would dare murder a holy nun? This is the primary question I struggled with as I began writing this book. Most authors begin a book with a clear idea of who did the deed and why. My writing process begins by forming the characters, putting them into a unique situation, and letting them work out the problems until they find the solution. It took the characters in Susanna most of the book before they discovered the truth: four characters had both motive and means to do away with an unusually abrasive nun. Who would dare murder a holy nun? You may be surprised!

The majority of nuns I encountered while attending Catholic grammar school were truly blessed women of God. They wore their black robes with dignity and pride. Just the sight of those long flowing robes with the starched white wimples surrounding their stern faces demanded respect from the most unruly student. I especially cherish the memory of Sister Mary Angela, my seventh grade teacher, who could rocket an eraser from the front of the room to the last row and nail a trouble maker on his shoulder with enough force to make his arm go numb. "Sign her up for the Yankee's!" we used to whisper. Nobody dared to ask her how she developed that arm of steel.

Prologue

Pete Patterson, the neighborhood paperboy, knocked on the back door of Taylor's home. Hannah, the housekeeper, purse in hand, opened the door.

"Morning, Petey."

"This is Saturday, Miss Hannah. I came yesterday to collect. Friday is collection day. It is important."

"I know, Petey. It's important. Here is your money for delivering the newspaper."

"But I came yesterday. Nobody came to the door. Friday is collection day. It is important."

Hannah sighed. She wondered how she might explain the problem in terms the mentally handicapped boy could understand.

"Sometimes Mrs. Taylor does a lot of sleeping on Fridays. Mrs. Taylor gets sad on Fridays and she sleeps so she won't have to remember about Amilee's death. You do remember, Petey, that Amilee died on a Friday?"

"Amilee! She's pretty. I love her!"

"Yes, everybody loved Amilee. But now she is in heaven and her mom is very sad, especially on Fridays."

Petey's round face grew solemn as he thought things over.

"But why doesn't anybody come to the door on Fridays? It is collection day, an important day."

Hannah sighed and patted his hand. "Listen now, Petey, this is important too. No one answers your knock because Mr. Taylor goes to work. Mrs. Taylor is sad and sleeping. And I'm not here on Fridays. It is my day off. Can you understand this?"

He nodded but the housekeeper still noticed puzzlement clouding his eyes.

"Petey. Can you come on Saturdays instead to collect? Or maybe even Thursday when I will be here to pay you? I know it is important to collect the money for the paper."

The boy nodded, then swiped at his face beneath the ball cap. Sweat trickled down his round cheeks. Hannah could not be sure if Petey grasped her careful explanation or not.

In a complete change of subject, Petey said, "It is hot today. Good thing my friends gave me some Mountain Dew."

As he unscrewed the top off the plastic bottle, Hannah caught a whiff of something stronger than soda pop. Instinct made her lunge for the bottle and snatch it away from the astonished boy.

"No! Don't drink this! It's not soda pop!"

Petey gasped. "But my friends told me it is Mountain Dew!"

Hannah tightened the cap and stared at the bottle, horrified.

"And who are these so-called friends?"

At her shrill tone, Petey stepped back. His eyes widened in fear.

"Joey and Clyde Kemper. They told me it was good for what ails me. What does that mean, Miss Hannah?"

"It means your friends are not very nice boys. They were trying to trick you, to make you sick. Did you drink any of it?"

He shook his head, mystified.

"Wait here. I'll bring you some real Mountain Dew."

As she handed him the aluminum can she explained. "See, Petey? Remember to only drink from soda cans, not from bottles. She this little tab on top? It's closed now. That means nobody opened it yet. It is safe for you to drink."

"No tricks?"

"Right! This can is just for you. It is safe."

The boy opened the snap tab and took a long swig. Hannah watched his throat open and close as he swallowed the cool drink. When the can was empty, he swiped his bare arm across his lips and grinned.

"Thanks Miss Hannah. See you next Friday."

Hannah smiled, shook her head and closed the door. She wondered, idly, why her voice never stammered or stuttered when she talked with the handicapped boy. *Maybe because he is a child of God, who never judges me or looks down on me as defective because I have trouble talking clearly to adults. Even if he doesn't remember about Fridays, he still treats me with respect.*

As Hannah walked into the kitchen to pour the contents of the green plastic bottle down the sink, she paused. *Maybe I should* ask *Mr. Taylor about changing my day off from Friday to some other day of the week.* She stood staring down the open drain.

"Or maybe I could work every day. Easier to keep an eye on Mayree."

She heaved a long sigh. Mayree needed looking after, she knew. Not just six days a week, but every day. *That sister of hers, Sister Susanna! I swear she will be the death of my Mayree if she keeps it up.*

Hannah turned from the sink, bottle in hand. Her chin came up.

"No more Miss Silent Housekeeper," she muttered and shook her fist at the ceiling. "My Mayree needs me to protect her."

Hannah screwed the top back on the green bottle. Slowly she set it aside as another troubling thought wrinkled her brow. *And she is not the only one needing protection. Those Kemper boys! Trying to hurt Petey. I'll fix their wagons!*

Chapter 1

Sister Susanna

After Mass that Sunday, Susanna changed her clothing in the guest room of Taylor's big house. She shrugged as she stared around the well-appointed bedroom.

"A sin, all this space going to waste. Mayree and Royal don't need all this room now. Both of them rattling around in this mini-mansion, just the two of them since Amilee died."

She shook her head, determined to speak to Royal about it. Susanna marched out of the bedroom and stomped down the long stairway to the main floor. A prolonged search of the downstairs proved fruitless. No Royal. She couldn't even find her sister, Mayree. Susanna huffed her way up the stairs again and started opening doors. Master bedroom, empty. After a second glance, she entered the room. Minutes later she resumed her search for her sister. All three bathrooms, unoccupied. It wasn't until she tried the bedroom previously belonging to her niece, Amilee, that she found her sister, deep in prayer.

Susanna stood in the doorway, watching as Mayree fingered a child's rosary. Eyes closed against the tears raining down her haggard face, Mayree's lips moved as she repeated the ritual prayers. One Our Father, ten Hail Mary's, followed by a Glory Be, then the decade repeated until all five sets of rosary prayers were completed.

The sight of her sister praying so fervently, bitter mourning etched into new lines of sorrow on her face, riled Susanna's temper until it boiled over.

"What are you doing, Mayree?"

Hands on her hips, she glared at her grieving sibling. Marching into the room, she stooped to snatch up the child's rosary that had slipped from Mayree's hands when surprised by her sister's shouting.

"I am praying! What does it look like I'm doing? Give me Amilee's rosary." She stood up on shaky legs and tried to grab the prayer beads. "That is my daughter's First Communion rosary. Give it to me, now!"

Susanna shook her head and backed away from her sister's frantic fingers as Mayree struggled to recover the rosary.

"No! You don't *deserve* to pray on this blessed rosary. Look at you! Crying and carrying on as if Amilee's death was a curse from God, instead of a blessing!"

Mayree gasped. "A blessing? A *blessing!* What is blessed about my only child being snatched from my arms at such an early age? Surely even a jealous God is not that cruel!"

Sister Susanna folded her arms across her chest and drew a deep righteous breath.

"You should be giving praise and thanksgiving for a *benevolent* God who took your daughter home to heaven, rather than allow her to suffer here on earth at the hands of evil men!"

Both women fell silent as they remembered what a tortuous hell Amilee went through before she died. Mayree sobbed into her open hands.

Susanna bit her lips to keep them from trembling. "Believe me, Mayree, I am doing this for your own good."

Mayree's head snapped up. "For my own good? *For my own good!* Just like you ran away from home and left me alone with *him*? Was that for my own good, too, Susanna?"

Mayree folded her arms against the sobs rising from her heaving chest. She glared at her older sibling. "Or was your running away to the safety of the convent for *your own good*? Did you even think about me, left behind, an innocent child at the mercy of an evil man? Did you even pray for me, Susanna?"

The nun sniffed. "I pray for all sinners, Mayree."

Susanna didn't intend her reply to come out sounding so haughty. She knew from the stiffness of her own neck muscles that she must look too righteous or something, because Mayree's face darkened with outrage. Before Susanna could say another word, her sister opened her right hand and gave the nun a hard slap across the face.

"Well this *sinner* wants her dead daughter's rosary back. Give it to me, now, or I'll call your convent and put in a formal complaint against you, for theft of a holy relic."

"Lot's of luck with that, Sis. A complaint from a woman half-mad with grief would hold no power over me at the convent."

Susanna tucked the rosary in her clothing, turned and stomped away. She noticed Hannah listening in the hallway outside the room. She scowled as she read the elderly housekeeper's thoughts written so plainly on her wrinkled face.

Poor Mayree, that sister of hers needs a good thrashing.

"You are not doing Mayree any good by coddling her, you know, Hannah. My sister needs to straighten up and move on!"

The housekeeper's hands tightened into fists as if she had to restrain herself from tackling the nun, forcing her onto the carpet, and prying Amilee's rosary out of Susanna's mean, clutching fingers.

"I wouldn't try that, Hannah. For one thing, I outweigh you. I've fought tougher people than you in my high school classroom, back in the day."

Susanna sniffed and straightened her shoulders. "Did you really intend to strike a holy woman of God? Be careful Hannah. You may lose your soul with that temper of your's."

Hannah still might have tried to force a confrontation, Susanna knew, but the heartbroken sobs from Mayree called her into the bedroom instead. The nun watched from the doorway as the housekeeper hurried to Mayree's side and hugged her. They rocked back and forth on the edge of the bed, decorated with a Tweety Bird comforter. It took long minutes before their sobs grew quiet. From the expressions on their faces, Susanna knew neither woman could find enough mercy in their hearts to forgive a well-meaning nun for her carelessly cruel words, especially the part about *thanking God!* for Amilee's death.

Later, Hannah failed to hide her satisfaction when the nun inquired about the absence of food on the table at supper time.

"Mr. Taylor is-sss playing golf. He usually eats at the ccc-clubhouse. Mayree is asleep. No reason for me to ccc-cook anything tonight."

Thanks to you, remained unspoken, but Susanna read the spiteful thought on Hannah's mulish expression.

"Mayree needs to consult a professional about her depression. Her drinking and taking sedatives every day cannot be good for her."

Susanna might as well have been talking to the air, because Hannah had disappeared

Chapter 2

Sister Susanna

Monday afternoon, Susanna frowned as she paged through the ledger on her desk. Monsignor McGaffee had asked her for help with the church's bookkeeping. Something had been amiss. Collections were up, a reflection of the increased people in the pews, parishioners now coming back to the Sacraments. The Pastor of St. Peter and Paul church insisted this welcome change was due to the forgiving nature of the new man in Rome. Pope Francis, a holy and saintly man, insisted pastors gather up all those forgotten sinners who had strayed away from Mother Church. Yet, despite the heavier collection baskets, the total dollar amount from donations and offerings dwindled each week.

Susanna thumbed through the stacks of dollars, all of them bundled in white bank bands stamped in black numbers: $500.

"Good thing I noticed Royal toss in a hundred dollar bill on Sunday."

There were no bills of that denomination in any of the banded stacks. Sister heaved a long sigh. *Sticky fingers. I thought it had to be either an usher or one of the money counters, but then the true culprit snuck into the church to revisit the scene of the crime. Gotcha!* Susanna thought and grinned.

She felt a headache stabbing behind her left eye. Susanna purely hated to relay upsetting news to her friend and mentor, Sean Mc-Gaffee. But the pastor had insisted Sister be totally truthful if she discovered any irregularities in the money count. She heaved another long sigh as she swept a separate bundle of loose bills into the top drawer to show Sean.

Later. Right now she needed to take something for her throbbing headache.

She leaned over to grab up her purse from under the desk. No purse?

She stood up so quickly her head spun.

"First the hundred dollar bill, now my purse?"

She wondered briefly if she had accidentally forgotten her purse in the pew after morning Mass. *No, I distinctly remember opening my purse to drop donations into the rosary collection box before I left church.* Susanna frowned again as she contemplated what she discovered that morning.

Sean will be livid when I tell him what is going on.

She stormed through the rectory, headed for the kitchen.

"Kat! What in the living hell is going on around here?"

Father's elderly housekeeper jumped at the sound of Sister's voice. She turned from the kitchen counter, chopping knife held in front of her for protection. Her faded gray eyes flashed quick anger as she stared at Susanna's crimson face. She waved the knife, pointing it at her.

"My name is Kathleen! Or Mrs. T. I do not answer to Kat!"

"But I heard Monsignor call you Kat!"

The elderly housekeeper's chin came up. "Monsignor is my boss. He can call me whatever he wants to. *You* are a *volunteer!* Not even an employee like me. My name is Kathleen!"

The haughty tone of the old woman's voice, the sharp knife she used to gesture toward Susanna, made her take an involuntary step backward.

She lowered the shrill tone of her voice. "Put down that knife, *Kathleen.* Or do you plan on using it on a nun?"

Her voice dripped with disdain. Implied in its tone was the very real possibility that old women who waved knives, especially at a *nun*, were in danger of damning their souls to everlasting hellfire.

"Oh, sorry Sister. I thought I heard shouting. I thought …"

Susanna crossed her arms and tapped her finely clad shoe.

"Yes, I was shouting, and no, I didn't come here to hurt you. For heaven's sake, Kat, put down that knife."

The knife clattered into the sink. The housekeeper's wrinkled face did not lose its outrage. Her trembling fingers reached up to brush aside an irritating strand of gray-tinged hair straggling against the side of her face. Her chin came up as her eyes flashed her inner thoughts, *I will not be shouted down by a bossy nun!*

Susanna tapped her foot again. "It's just that … Never mind. Have you seen my purse?"

Kathleen pointed toward the end of the counter.

"You dumped it there when you came through this morning. I haven't touched it."

The housekeeper stared at her feet. A slow flush spread across her face. Susanna realized the old woman felt insulted by her harsh words. She almost apologized, but brushed aside the polite thought in her rush to examine the contents of her large black purse.

Nothing disturbed. Thank God!

"Thanks Kathleen."

She flung the comment over her shoulder, an overdue apology, too little too late. The bathroom door, just off the kitchen, slammed shut as she rushed inside.

Chapter 3

Kathleen

Kathleen stared at the closed bathroom door for long moments before she turned away to finish making the salad. A faint smile lifted the corners of her wrinkled lips, then faded. She glanced toward the bathroom door. Still closed. Kathleen had a good idea what mischief Sister Susanna was hiding behind that bland barrier.

She acts so holy and righteous, but inside, she is just a poor sinner like the rest of us.

Kathleen shook her head at the hypocrisy of some people who called themselves true Christians. She walked to the closed door and tapped on it.

"Are you staying for supper?"

"No! I'm going home."

Minutes later, rubbing her forehead and pleading a migraine, Sister Susanna escaped to the parking lot. Shortly after, Mrs. T heard the sound of squealing tires as the compact car roared out of the parking lot.

Chapter 4

Mayree and Royal

Monday evening, Mayree Taylor wondered briefly why her sister, Susanna Harrison, did not come home from her job at the rectory in time for the evening meal.

"Strange, Suzy never misses a meal! And it shows, too," she said.

Spite twisted her mouth into ugly lines as she remembered yesterday's quarrel.

"Why do we still bicker after all these years?"

She flushed as she mentally reviewed the bitterness that had tinged their quarrel. Hateful words, long buried since their troubled childhood, had spewed forth with an ugliness only close kin could remember and conjure up to suit those angry moments.

Mayree stiffened her spine. "I *won't* be insulted again, not by my own sister! I don't care if she is a nun, Susanna has no right to tell me to *thank God* for Amilee's death. It isn't her daughter who died so tragically just two months ago. How I grieve is my own business. Not hers! She never had a child of her own. How dare she tell me to stop crying over the loss of my only daughter!"

Across the length of the long dining room table, her husband, Royal, bowed his head. He said nothing as his wife ranted and raved about her sister. In his secret heart, he rejoiced as Mayree's tirade continued long and loud. *Finally! Maybe now Mayree will send her meddling sister home. Maybe then we can begin to heal.*

Mayree beckoned her housekeeper to serve the meal immediately.

"We won't wait for Susanna tonight, Hannah. I don't care if she comes home or not. Let her bend Father McGaffee's ear for a change. I'm sick of her meddling lectures."

Across the table, Royal glanced at his wife's stony face and picked up his napkin. Without comment, he spread the cloth across his lap. They ate their meal in silence.

Sister Susanna did not return to their home that night at all.

Chapter 5

Hannah

Hannah, Taylor's housekeeper worked silently in the kitchen. Her wrinkled old hands trembled as she washed up the pots and pans used for the preparation of their evening meal. One ear tilted toward the dining room, she heaved a long sigh at the lack of conversation between Mayree and Royal.

It just ain't right, those two not talking at all. Little Amilee has been gone a few months now, yet her parents still aren't turning to each other for comfort. Hannah shook her head and reached for a drying towel. She feared for their marriage, she truly did.

And that Sister Susanna! That sharp tongued nun! She needs a good shaking to bring her down off that high horse she prances around on. Hannah ducked her head and scowled into the sink. She wished fervently for the return of the happiness that had flooded this house before Amilee had been found dead in the garage. Susanna had come up from Biloxi to "comfort" her sister, Mayree. *Scant comfort from that old biddy! She should be ashamed to even be called a nun. Nuns were supposed to be sweet and holy.* At least that's what Hannah had heard from her Catholic kin. But Hannah had been raised by an assortment of relatives after her parents died in an automobile accident when the girl was six. None of the various kin, obviously reluctant to raise an orphan child who was moody and shy and sometimes difficult to understand, even went to church. Now, in her late fifties, Hannah still stuttered when she felt backed into a corner by anyone in authority.

That Sheriff Lance Lundrum, he scares the be-jesus out of me, she thought.

"No way in hell will I talk to the Sheriff about all the thievery going on around here."

Chapter 6

The Newlyweds

Late that Monday afternoon, Lance rolled over on the beach blanket, braced his bulky frame on one elbow, and stared down at his new bride.

"Lorena, my beloved wife, you are more beautiful than ever. I am the most blessed of men in this tired old world."

Lorena shaded her eyes and grinned. "Maybe it is you who are tired today, hmmm? Too much night life for an old duffer like you?"

They tussled playfully on the sandy beach. It ended with a long kiss, made even sweeter by the shocking pull of the Atlantic ocean's powerful waves breaking across their feet. They broke apart, laughing.

"Better move this blanket, Sweetheart, before we get carried away by the tide."

"And what tide would you be talking about, Lance?"

He swept her up into his arms and kissed her thoroughly. He loved the way she changed so completely from her usual serious, never-let-them-see-you-smile, mortician and Coroner of Colquitt County, Georgia, to this teasing imp whose arms hugged his neck. Her long dark hair hung over his arm as she tilted her face toward the sky and laughed into the sunshine.

After a storybook wedding and a huge reception at the old Wilton mansion, they had honeymooned at the Outer Banks of North

Carolina. It had been a week of sweet surprises, made even more special as they fell asleep to the comforting sounds of breaking waves outside their rented cabin. It had been a week of deep love making, unfettered by any serious thoughts about back home or their work responsibilities. Tomorrow they would pack up and go home.

Lorena struggled to be let down from his burly arms. She stooped to pick up an orange mesh bag half hidden by their blanket. The mesh bag had originally contained big juicy naval oranges from California.

"Can't forget the beach shells for John-Duncan."

Lorena had developed a hankering for oranges while staying in their cabin on the shore. Lance grinned as he thought of the un-counted trips he made to a local Lion King to replenish her sudden craving for fresh oranges.

Shaking the mesh bag, now full of shells that had washed up on the beach, Lorena sighed at the thought of flying back to Georgia. She did miss her special needs son, John-Duncan, but Belle, her live in housekeeper and loving caregiver for her son, kept things running smoothly at their apartment above McGee's Mortuary.

Lance watched the changing patterns on his beloved wife's face. He read the real regret there.

"You having mixed thoughts about going home, Lorena?"

She nodded. "This has been such a special week. Just us, alone together. I miss John-Duncan, of course, but ..."

She tousled his thick hair. He hugged her.

"I know, Darlin'. Back to business. The criminals and the newly dead won't wait on a couple of love-sick pups like us."

They giggled together as they showered the sand off their sun-bronzed bodies.

They enjoyed a domestic half hour preparing supper at the cabin, made even more special because they worked together in the tiny kitchen. Elbow to elbow, they cooked pasta and heated a jar of spaghetti sauce. They dished it up on paper plates and dug in. Lance grinned at his new wife's ravenous appetite.

"Eating for two now, Darlin'?" he said.

She glanced up, a smear of red sauce on her full lips, and giggled.

"You know it! Starved all the time now."

He reached across and swiped at her lips with a paper napkin.

"Love to see a healthy woman enjoying her grub," he rumbled. His love for her gleamed in his deep brown eyes.

They went to bed early. Flight time tomorrow morning, eleven o'clock.

At five a.m. the next morning, Lance's cell phone rang. He rolled over and snapped on the table lamp. Blinking, he scowled at Keith's name on the display. Keith Davis was his new deputy. He had been appointed just before Lorena and Sheriff Lance Lundrum left on their honeymoon.

Lance groaned as he opened the phone.

"Hellfire, Lorena! They can't even wait till we get home to start hounding us."

Chapter 7

Mayree

Tuesday morning, Royal had already left for his office by the time Mayree dragged herself into the shower. She had to lean against the wall to steady herself as the water blasted shampoo down her back.

Those darn sedatives. They make me feel like an addict waking up to another hopeless day. Not really living. Barely existing, until it's time to take another pill or sneak another drink just to make it through the day without my baby girl. God, will I ever feel hope or contentment again?

Hannah had already spread out an outfit for her to wear. She stood quietly, just outside the bedroom door, ready to help Mayree in any way. Hannah had come to live with them over twelve years ago. Mayree, carrying the child who would become Amilee, needed bed rest during most of her pregnancy. The housekeeper had been a God-send at the time. Now Mayree wondered if she should quietly dismiss her longtime friend and caregiver. Just looking as Hannah's sorrowful face each day reminded her of their loss, and somehow even seemed to intensify her own grief. *No, Hannah stays. I need her now more than ever.*

"Breakfast this morning, Mmm-may?"

Mayree felt no hunger, but the hopeful expression on her friend's face made her nod agreement, if a tad reluctantly.

"Good! I ss-set the table already."

Mayree sat down and glanced at the second plate on the table. She wondered if it was for Royal or for her sister, Susanna. *No matter,* she thought bleakly. *I won't be talking to either of them this morning.* Stubbornness firmed up her chin. She glanced up as Hannah placed a platter of scrambled eggs and toast in front of her.

"Hannah, I plan to tell my sister to go home today. Can I count on you to back me up on this?"

Hannah patted her gently.

"Mm-may. You know I am on your sss-side, no matter what. But I think you won't have that ccc-conversation after all."

"Oh?"

Hannah smiled.

"She didn't come home last night. Mm-maybe she already left for Biloxi."

And good riddance!

Hannah didn't need to say it out loud. Mayree could read it on her puckered face. She grinned and echoed the thought.

"Yes, and good riddance."

The women grinned at each other in complete agreement. Both glanced up, surprised, as Royal walked into the room.

Chapter 8

Royal

Royal approached his wife, sitting at the table, just finishing her breakfast coffee. He dreaded being the messenger of bad news yet another time. Hannah watched him, alarmed at whatever she saw on his face. The housekeeper turned to make her escape, but Royal stopped her with a word.

"Wait! Hannah, we might need you ..."

His voice sounded puny even as he spoke. Royal cleared his throat.

"I mean ... oh hell, Mayree. There's just no easy way to tell you this. Your sister died in an automobile accident. Must have happened sometime late last evening, Keith told me. Susanna wrapped her car around a tree. Wreck wasn't found until early this morning."

He stopped, out of breath, and waited for his wife's reaction. It was not what he expected, not at all.

Mayree smiled. She dusted off her fingers in a dismissive gesture.

Eyes reflecting a strange satisfaction, she said, "Good riddance!"

Chapter 9

Keith Davis

Keith hated to call Sheriff Lundrum while he was on his honeymoon, but the death of Sister Susanna just seemed wrong somehow. It looked like an accidental death since she had wrapped her car around a tree, but his hackles rose as he bent over the still and bloody form. He smelled alcohol! *Do nuns even drink?* He pondered about it as he waited for the ambulance.

An early morning sanitary worker had spotted the wreck from his perch on the back of the garbage truck. Keith, jerked out of bed, responded to the report of a automobile accident on Rectory Drive He squirmed now, trying to stay awake as he sat in the official Sheriff's car. He yawned and drummed his fingers on the steering wheel. *Dark outside, still. Should I call Lance now, or wait until daylight?* He worried about calling his boss so early, but in truth, he wasn't sure just what to do.

Screwing up his courage, he picked up his cell and made the call. After speaking to Lance, he had orders to schedule an autopsy. Lorena got on the line.

"And Keith, don't let Mother Superior from Susanna's Order push you around. Those old nuns insist that any member of their community must be buried within 24 hours, without embalming or anything that disturbs the *holy* corpse."

Keith grinned. "Like discovering cause of death, you mean, Lorena?"

"Exactly. As Coroner of Colquitt County, I am officially ordering an autopsy."

Lance's deep voice rumbled over the phone line.

"See you tomorrow, Keith. Hold down the fort."

Keith did not appreciate that bit of stern advice until he dealt with Sister Ann Mary, Mother Superior of The Merciful Sisters of the Mother of God.

Chapter 10

Lance

Lance unbuckled his seat belt once their small plane reached cruising height. He leaned forward to gaze fondly at his beautiful wife.

Asleep already? He grinned as he remembered how quickly and how deeply his new wife slipped into slumber these days. *Must be the baby draining her energy*, he thought, smiling to himself. He stared at the tiny mound swelling her lower abdomen. He ached to reach over and stroke the tiny baby bump, physical evidence of their child growing within her. Lorena had mentioned that she hoped the baby would be a boy, a son for her virile husband, proof of his manhood. But Lance, in his secret heart kept well hidden from all and sundry, prayed the child would be a little girl. Just the thought of a daughter, as beautiful and as kind-hearted as her mother, made his throat thick with emotion. He brushed at his eyes, sweeping away the sweet tears of his dreams for their future. Just in time.

Lorena awoke. Her smile made his heart leap for joy. Unaware of the grinning people in adjoining seats, he swept her into his arms for a long hug.

"Lorena, Darlin', I just love you so much."

She laughed against his shoulder, and patted him like a new mother burps an oversized baby. People were staring at them. She closed her eyes against their shocked and disapproving glares of consternation. She kissed him long and deeply.

"Love you too, my wild and woolly husband," she said.

She gently shoved him back toward his seat. Lance sensed a *but* coming on.

"But, maybe we should save all these hugs and kisses for our private time together?"

Lance sank back into his seat like a harpooned whale.

"Now, Lorena Darlin', I know how you value your privacy, but I waited so long for us to marry… I just can't help myself sometimes."

She patted his big paw and smiled to soften the blow as she patiently explained why they needed to act more formally toward each other in public places.

"Now Lance, you do know we are in a challenging situation? You are the Sheriff. I am the Coroner. We have to act like professionals when we come together, working to solve the mysterious deaths that happen now and then in Colquitt County."

"I know, Darlin' but …" He couldn't keep the miseries out of his voice.

"I know we are husband and wife now, Lance. But our duties require that we forget all the huggy and kissy stuff when we are working together. At home in the bedroom? Oh, yeah! Let it rip, the hotter the better. But not in public. OK?"

Lance heaved a long sigh and squirmed against the back of his too narrow airline seat.

"Maybe it's time one of us retires!" he muttered.

Lorena's face darkened. She turned away without another word, crossed her arms across her chest, and shortly thereafter she slipped into another deep sleep.

Chapter 11

Monsignor Sean McGaffee

"Now young man, you just listen to me!"

Monsignor glanced down from his lofty height at the tiny and very determined nun standing beside him. He secretly admired her spunk, but had to hide a smile at the crimson fury flushing her face. *You are fighting a losing battle, Sister Ann Mary,* he thought. *The Sheriff's bulldog will not budge an inch.*

Sister Ann Mary, Mother Superior of the Order, had been driven up from Biloxi that morning by a fourth year seminarian, Michael Francis. Sean noticed the young deacon as he waited in the driveway. Neatly dressed in dark slacks, white short sleeved shirt and navy tie, the cleanly shaven man leaned against the white panel truck. He folded well-muscled arms across his chest as he watched, from a safe distance, the argument between the petite old nun and the Sheriff's deputy.

Sean smiled and ducked his head. Sister Ann Mary fully intended to retrieve Sister Susanna's holy remains, he realized. Her determined little chin reminded Monsignor of all the teaching nuns he had been forced to bow respectfully to during his school years. Beneath her long black habit, a small pointed-toe black shoe tapped impatiently.

"You *will* give over the body of Sister Susanna to me. Now!"

Keith Davis, the Sheriff's deputy (*fondly labeled his bulldog for his size, determination and strength of will*) folded his arms and leaned against the front door of Lorena McGee's Funeral Mortuary. The door was locked and it seemed obvious to the Pastor that the tall burly man did not intend to unlock it for anyone. Neither determined nun, nor an imposing figure like himself, a Monsignor of the Holy Roman Catholic Church, could sway Deputy Davis from his official duties.

"Sorry, Sister. I have my orders from the Coroner. Susanna's death occurred under suspicious circumstances. There must be an autopsy. State law."

Sean was not pleased by this turn of events. Not only had the parish lost a good woman, a nun who dedicated her life to the service of the Church, but Sister Susanna was a close friend. She had worked hard to unlock the financial mysteries of his parish. When he had returned from a sick call yesterday, he found the note Susanna left on his desk.

Sean, I believe I found our thief. Talk to you tomorrow.

Now she was dead, of *suspicious circumstances.*

"But what about Church law?" Sean said

Keith turned to him with a frown.

"Father, even Church law does not apply in this instance. There has to be an autopsy."

"When will they be back from their honeymoon?"

"Their plane should be landing right about now."

Monsignor tapped his watch.

"Another hour or so until they drive down here."

And Lorena will be too exhausted to work on the body tonight, Sean thought.

He turned to the fuming Mother Superior.

"Ann Mary, can't this wait until tomorrow? Susanna won't be any deader tomorrow than she is right now."

"But our Order's rules ..."

"Will have to be waived this time. Sorry, Sister."

Keith looked relieved as he walked back to his police car. He did offer the difficult nun a ride but she waved him off impatiently. "I have a driver!"

Monsignor lightly touched her arm. "Sister Ann Mary, you both will need overnight accommodations." He gestured toward the waiting Michael Francis. "You and your driver are both welcome to stay with me until the Coroner releases the holy remains. Plenty of room in the rectory."

Fuming, Ann Mary shook her head hard enough to dislodge her white wimple. Snatching at the old fashioned face-framing head gear, she straightened it, tucked in an errant gray curl with a sharp hat pin, and stomped her feet.

"Really Monsignor! You should know better! A nun cannot spend a night alone with a priest, no matter how big your parsonage might be! Isn't there a motel or a convent nearby where I could sleep tonight?"

Sean covered his grin with a sudden coughing fit. He pointed to the end of the driveway.

"You could always stay with Susanna's relatives. Royal Taylor is waiting, in case you needed anything. His wife Mayree is Susanna's closest kin, her only sister."

Ann Mary looked confused. "But what about Michael Francis? Where will he stay?"

Sean dared to pat the fuming nun's blue-veined hand.

"That young man can stay with me in the rectory."

Mollified, Sister Ann Mary whirled around and sailed her dark habit down the driveway.

Royal Taylor leaned against his flashy Corvette, arms crossed as he waited. As soon as the elderly nun approached, he opened the passenger door and helped her fall into the low front seat.

Monsignor stepped away from the mortuary door. He beckoned the seminarian and gave him instructions to the rectory by way of nearby country roads.

"I'm going to walk home," he said. "Need to clear my head on this terrible thing."

He gestured toward the woods path that led from McGee's Funeral Home, through the public graveyard and to his parsonage.

"You go ahead, Mr. Francis. I will probably be back at the rectory before you find it."

Praying the young man wouldn't get lost, Sean turned toward the path. He bent over, hands clenched behind his back. Monsignor had always been proud of his tall imposing posture. Now, pride forgotten, he walked slowly, his body bowed with sorrow as he shuffled through the woods path that divided McGee's cemetery from his rectory and church a quarter mile away. His shiny black shoes kicked up leaf mold as he scuffed his feet down the path.

Suddenly he remembered that Lorena McGee had been kidnaped and assaulted as she walked along this very path, just a few months earlier. Her attacker, a sneaky local moonshiner, had been caught by the Sheriff and the F.B.I. He was serving hard time in Federal prison now, *thank God!* Sean prayed for his soul every day, as he did for any person who had fallen under Satan's wicked spell. But in his secret heart, Monsignor felt relief that a mean spiteful man was now safely locked away.

He sighed. Glancing around absently, he noticed how bare the deciduas trees looked, their branches dark against the mild blue sky. *Late autumn now, winter coming on fast.* He shivered and pulled his coat collar snug against the back of his regal neck. He needed this uncomfortable walk to clear his muddled thoughts.

Stealing money from the collection is one thing, a minor sin. But deliberately killing a nun? Guilt pierced his soul like an icy knife. *If only I hadn't brought Susanna in to audit the financial books, maybe she would be alive today.*

Troubled, his mind reviewing his parishioners and their possible sins, he fished out a rosary and prayed his way home.

Chapter 12

Royal Taylor

Keith had notified Royal Taylor about the death of Sister Susanna mid-morning on Tuesday. The District Attorney had been at his office in Oakhill. Shocked, he promised to go home immediately to break the news to Mayree.

After Keith spoke with the Sheriff again, Lance called Royal.

"I think you might better hightail it over to Lorena's mortuary, Royal. Keith might need some official backup and moral support when he deals with the wrath of Mother Superior."

Lance's deep chuckle echoed over the phone. "Lorena tells me nothing is fiercer than an old nun determined to have her own way, regardless!"

Royal had waited and watched from the safe end of the driveway as the tiny nun shook her fist and shouted. His mind wandered back to the scene at home when he told his wife that her sister was dead. It did astonish him when Mayree smiled at the news.

Good riddance! she said. Royal still pondered about that. Of course the sisters had that vicious quarrel on Sunday, but still ...*No fireworks this time,* he thought, relieved. *Guess Susanna really wore out her welcome if even her sister refused to mourn her tragic death. Mayree even looked relieved!*

A nagging little doubt made him wonder at his wife's lack of sympathy. Had Mayree done something ...? He shrugged and refused to even think about it anymore.

When Sister Ann Mary turned to stomp down the driveway, Royal leaped to open the passenger door for the angry nun.

Royal slid a long glance toward the fuming nun sitting beside him. He purposely lowered the speed of his high-powered sport's car after she grabbed the door handle in a panic when he sped away from the Funeral Home.

"You don't need to drive like the hounds of hell are after us, young man!" she said tartly.

"Yes Ma'am."

"Yes, *Sister!* I am not a Ma'am, I am a nun!"

"Yes Ma ... I mean, yes Sister!"

Royal rolled his eyes then deliberately kept his gaze straight ahead. No need to meet *Sister's* gaze. He could feel her outrage without turning his head. It burned against his cheek like the bite from a fire-ant.

"I suppose you are a friend of that impertinent hoodlum back there?"

Royal hid a grin. He shook his head and dared to venture an explanation.

"Deputy Davis is employed by the Sheriff. As District Attorney of Colquitt County, I sometimes need his help in a murder investigation. But ..."

"*Murder investigation!*"

He jumped. Who would believe a tiny nun could screech like that? Raised the hackles on his neck, that shriek did for sure. He ducked as Sister Ann Mary continued her high-pitched verbal protest.

"Murder? Murder! Who would *dare* murder a blessed woman like Sister Susanna?"

Royal, brother-in-law of the so-called blessed woman, knew plenty of people who wouldn't mind getting rid of that big mouthed, holier-than-thou nun, *including his wife, Susanna's sibling.* Wisely, he kept his mouth shut.

Sister Ann Mary leaned back in the seat. Her fingers laced together fiercely as if she prayed not to the Higher Power, but to all the wicked demons of earth.

"Ridiculous!" she muttered.

She slid another hot glance toward Royal. He ignored her, saying a silent prayer that this nightmare would end tomorrow, after the autopsy.

If I never have to look at another nun the rest of my days, it would be fine with me!

Royal dared to mention his fervent wish.

"I hope this whole mess will soon be over, Sister. For all our sakes."

They rode the rest of the way home in silence.

Hannah, their housekeeper, glared as she opened the front door. *Pretty obvious Hannah dislikes this nun too,* he thought. Royal coughed to cover a chuckle as he pointed to the living room. He did not touch the prickly old harridan, merely gestured.

"This way, Mother Superior. I am sure Hannah will bring you some refreshments if you need something to sustain you until dinner."

"No, thank you, Mr. Taylor. I just need a quiet place to pray my rosary."

The old nun, dark robes flaring, sailed into the living room, chose the most uncomfortable seat available, and sank into it with an exhausted sigh. A long black rosary appeared as if conjured up by a holy magician. Sister made the Sign of the Cross, kissed the crucifix, and bent her head as she silently prayed.

Royal glanced at Hannah as she lingered beside him. The housekeeper stared at the elderly nun. Her eyes expressed alarm as the rosary beads appeared in the wrinkled old hands. When Royal touched Hannah's arm, she jumped. He gestured to the hallway. Hannah stepped back. She met his gaze with visible reluctance.

"What is it, Hannah?" he whispered.

She shook her head and stared at the floor.

Royal's training as District Attorney flared.

"Something about the rosary? Is that it? Hannah, you looked scared to death when you saw Sister bring it out."

Hannah grew so pale, he feared for her heart. He touched her hand to comfort her. She leaped back so quickly, she stumbled and almost fell. Royal grabbed her arm and steered her into his den, a few steps away. He closed the door behind them and pointed to a chair in front of his desk. Royal conducted most of his business affairs at the office in Oakhill, but he did have occasion to question suspects here in his own home. He put on his stern D.A. face and stared hard at his housekeeper.

"Now Hannah. You know something. I can read it in your face. Tell me!"

Hannah's eyes filled with tears. She shook her head. When she finally opened her mouth to speak, she stuttered so badly, Royal felt a wave of sympathy wash over him.

"Itttttt's just thaaaaaat." Hannah shrugged and spread her hands in hopeless defeat.

"The rosary? Something about the rosary?" he prodded gently.

Hannah nodded. He waited, but the woman's lips seemed glued together by her speech impediment.

"Now, just tell me this, Hannah. Does it have anything to do with Susanna's death?"

Hannah glanced at him with fervent relief. She shook her head slowly and spread her hands.

"I dooooooooon't think ssss so."

Royal sighed and leaned against his desk.

"Can you write out what you mean about the rosary? What frightened you when you saw Mother Superior praying it just now?"

Hannah nodded. She reached for a pen on the desk. Royal tore off a sheet from a yellow legal pad and handed it to her. She bent over her work. Moments later she straightened up and handed both paper and pen to him.

Amilee's rosary is missing. Miss Mayree used to pray it every day in Ami's room.

Royal glanced up, surprised. "Really, Hannah? I never knew this."

Hannah nodded. She pointed toward the paper. He slid it toward her, along with the pen.

Mayree spends a long time in Amilee's room every day. Sunday, while you were out golfing, that sister of her's, that Sister Susanna, found her there. They had a terrible shouting time of it. Susanna took Amilee's rosary!

Hannah put down the pen and shook her head. She folded her arms across her chest.

Case closed, he thought. *No use asking Hannah any more questions. She is closed for business right now, maybe forever.* He sighed.

"So, now Amilee's rosary is missing? You say Susanna took it?"

Hannah nodded and stared at the floor.

Royal thought, *It's obvious that Susanna took the rosary away so Mayree wouldn't "dwell on her sorrow and loss."* He had heard those very words from that meddlesome nun several times in the past few weeks. Anger flared behind his eyes, a crimson flash that almost blinded him. The *injustice* of it all. A childless nun trying to tell, no *order!* his grieving wife to stop weeping over the loss of their only child.

"Thanks Hannah," he said as he hurried out the door. He suddenly felt an urgent need to find his wife and give her a long hug.

Chapter 13

The Homecoming

John-Duncan met his mother at the top step of their apartment above McGee's Mortuary. His fierce hug almost sent both of them tumbling back down the stairway. Thankfully, Lance, carrying suitcases, stiffened quickly and grabbed mother and son before tragedy struck.

Lorena gasped as she regained her balance. She stumbled a bit before Lance managed to half lift, half shove her into the hall at the top of the long stairway. She laughed as she gently pushed John-Duncan out of her arms.

"John, really! I know you are happy to see us, but please remember the rules, no pushing people down the steps."

John-Duncan flapped his hands, still excited by his mother's return. Lorena grabbed them and leaned closer to plant a kiss on his cheek. She had to rise on tip-toe to reach him.

"Why, John, you must have grown another couple of inches while we were gone. Pretty soon I'll need a ladder to even pat your face."

The boy/man beamed.

"Grandma Belle says I eat enough to grow two people instead of just me."

Belle appeared behind him. "And Johnny is right! He just keeps growing."

Their housekeeper reached out hesitantly to accept Lorena's offered hug. Belle had been rescued from an abusive husband. She still felt shy about expressing emotion. But Lorena's warm ways were winning her over.

"Thank you so much for taking care of our son while we were gone, Belle. You are a treasure beyond compare."

"There you go, sounding like Doc Huey again."

But Belle smiled, her face flushed with pleasure at being so appreciated by her employer, who was now a dear friend.

"You folks hungry? I made meat loaf."

Lance, stowing the suitcases against the wall beside their bedroom door, turned with a huge grin spreading across his rugged face. "Cornbread too, I hope?"

"Wouldn't be a righteous meal without cornbread, right Sheriff?"

"Now Belle," he rumbled in his deep voice. "You needn't call me Sheriff. Here at home, I am just plain Lance."

Belle surprised them all by saluting. "Yes, Sir, Mister Lance."

They laughed as they walked down the hall, arms around each other, marveling at the wondrous down home food smells wafting from the kitchen. Just before they folded their hands to say Grace, John-Duncan turned to his mother.

"What did you bring me, Mama?" His face glowed with the innocent greed of a child.

Lorena shook her napkin, laid it across her lap, and gestured for her son to do the same.

"Something very special, John. You will see, after supper. Now, let's eat. I am starved."

"Amen to that," Lance said and folded his hands for the Blessing Before Meals.

Chapter 14

Lorena

Lorena yawned as she gowned up for the autopsy of Sister Susanna Harrison.

Maybe I shouldn't have enjoyed that wonderful breakfast that Belle cooked for us this morning. Too much food always makes me sluggish. Even as the thought crossed her mind, Lorena grinned. It had only been an hour, but already she craved more food. *Must be the baby demanding to be fed. He probably takes after Lance. Big babies grow into big men, and big guys need to eat, pronto like, as Doc Huey always says.*

Lorena gently rubbed the tiny baby bump beneath her long rubber apron. Even in the grim setting of the autopsy room, her heart swelled with gratitude for the promise of a new life growing within her.

Doc Huey nudged her arm. "No time for day-dreaming today, Lorena, my dear. That fierce little nun is chomping at the bit to take this 'holy woman' back to their convent."

"Thanks Huey. I need waking up sometimes these days."

His faded brown eyes crinkled above the surgical mask. He nodded, his eyes shining.

"Miss your morning coffee, do you, my dear?"

She smiled fondly at the man who had been her friend since childhood.

"The small sacrifice of no coffee is not a big deal, as John-Duncan might say. But I do need extra time to wake up these days."

She patted her belly again.

"That's why I'm here for you, Lorena. You are a treasure beyond compare to me. I will do anything to help you out. You do know that?"

"Thanks Doc. Let's get to work."

She triggered the overhead microphone and snapped on her gloves. One on either side of the metal table, they began the autopsy. Lorena began by stating the time and date.

"Today we begin the autopsy of Sister Susanna Harrison, a nun affiliated with the Merciful Sisters of the Mother of God, from Biloxi Mississippi."

Gently, she lifted the white drape covering the nun's upper body and folded it across her lower abdomen. Doc Huey grunted as he studied the dark bruising across the body's upper chest area. A clear half circle above the breasts revealed the obvious cause of the bruises.

"Susanna sure hit that steering wheel pretty hard. Didn't the car have an air bag?"

Lorena shrugged and leaned over a chart beside the stainless steel table.

"Keith's notes don't mention a deflated air bag hanging from the steering wheel."

Doc softly swore. "Those old cheapskates down to Biloxi probably bought the smallest and least expensive automobile modal for the convent drivers to use. Some of those foreign make cars have a recall on their air bags. I read it just last week in the *Pea Picker News*."

Lorena used a scalpel to make an incision down the middle of the corpse's chest. She noticed an unusual amount of clotted blood in the chest cavity. Doc leaned over for a closer look. He gasped. His brown eyes grew wide with alarm. He pointed to an area deep within the revealed chest cavity.

"Hellfire, Lorena! Look at the hemorrhaging in her trachea and bronchial tubes!"

"Never saw anything like this, Doc. Caused by the violent impact of her body against the steering wheel when she hit that oak tree, you think?"

Doc shook his head and tore off his gloves. He stepped away from the table, his face mottled with rage. He began to pace to and fro within the white walls of Lorena's autopsy room. He shook his fist and cussed like a drunken sailor. Lorena had never seen Huey, her friend since way back when, so upset. She was shocked at his language and his anger.

"Haven't seen this since old Izzy Krampet died from sampling his own moonshine. Feds were after him so he took a long swig from his 'special blend' a super high octane brew made with rubbing alcohol as a kicker. Well it had a kicker all right. Killed old Izzy within a half hour. He passed out while trying to outrun the Revenuers. Hit a tree dead on, just like Susanna. Never knew what hit him."

Lorena stared again at the pools of clotted blood within the body before her. Her violet eyes reflected horror as she gazed at Doc Huey's wrinkled old face above the gauze mask. She leaned over the body as if to take a long sniff.

"Does she smell of alcohol, Doc?"

"Hellfire Lorena! Step back from that table! "

"What? Why?"

He rushed to her side, grabbed her around her waist and dragged her back toward the nearest wall.

"Even sniffing the vapors from Isopropanol can affect you, and your unborn baby!"

She clutched at her baby bump and burst into tears.

"Doc, do you think I hurt the baby by just being near those fumes?"

She ripped off her gloves and threw them onto the floor. Doc's big hand clutched her wrist to stop her from tearing off her mask, too.

"Lorena, Darling. You need this mask now to protect both of you. Thank God you put the exhaust fan on before we started cutting her open."

He stared wildly around the room at the shelves and closed cupboard doors.

"Don't happen to have one of those hepa-filter masks do you?"

Relief made her sag against him, then she straightened and rushed toward the last cupboard next to the steel door. Moments later, both she and Huey wore new protective masks. They gazed at each other and tried to smile.

"These new super-safe masks look like these bulky gas masks the soldiers wore during those old WWII movies."

"We're going to double glove on this job, Lorena."

She nodded, faint with relief. *Maybe I didn't harm the baby after all?* Doubt tickled her conscience. Lorena stared at the body on the table. *Maybe Lance is right? Is my job too dangerous now? If I hurt our baby in any way, I could never forgive myself.*

She stepped away from the table and stared long and hard at Huey.

"Can you can finish this autopsy without me, Doc? I …"

"Ah, Lorena. I can see the storm going on in your heart now. I think with these new fangled super-duper hifalutin' masks we should all be safe. But if you want, I can certainly finish up here. Go sit down outside somewhere. I will find you when I'm done."

He paused and reached for an extra pair of gloves.

"I am sorry for my bad language before. Such a sinful way for a holy woman to die."

He shook his head for long moments before gazing into Lorena's eyes. She paused at the door, her hand on the knob.

"But Doc, where did Susanna get moonshine? A smart woman like that, she must have known the risks of drinking home brew."

"What wonders me, Lorena, is this: do nuns even drink at all? I mean alcoholic drinks. I know, Communion wine and all that, but serious drinking? Is it possible, or even probable that she drank the moonshine deliberately?"

Lorena said, "Either that, or she was murdered."

They stared at each other. Long moments later, Lorena reminded Doc to remove the first CD recording of the autopsy and insert a new one.

"You are starting over from scratch, Doc," she said. Her voice wobbled. "I want to read Keith's report again. Did he find a canning jar or a bottle of shine in the wrecked car? Maybe a flask?"

"Lorena, my dear. You need to call in the D.A. on this."

She nodded grimly as she opened the steel door.

"What a scandal this would make for the *Pea Picker News*. The sister-in-law of Royal Taylor, District Attorney of Colquitt County, and a nun to boot, dead from an overdose of moonshine."

He shook his head, reached for new gloves and adjusted his mask.

"A sad day, Lorena."

Chapter 15

Raysa Elwood

Doc Huey looked terrible as he stumbled through the office door of his Health Clinic. His Physician's Assistant, Raysa, one of the Wilton sisters, glanced up. Her deep brown eyes, mirrors of his own, grew wide with concern.

"Huey! What happened? You look as if you saw a ghost just now."

She rushed over to his side, grabbed his sagging body, and urged him into the nearest comfortable chair.

"Raysa, Princess, I never thought I would live to see a day like this one." He shook his shaggy gray hair and stared around the empty office. Pointing to a nearby cupboard, he gulped and sighed. "Princess? Could you pour me a tad of something strong? I need some bucking up."

"What happened?" she said as she opened the nearly full bottle of Jack Daniels.

Doc took a long swig of the alcohol. He leaned back in the chair. It squeaked loudly as he heaved another long sigh.

"Ah Raysa, that poor nun ... She died from drinking moonshine." He shook his head. "Never thought this day would ever come, when even the holy women of the church take to drinking their problems away."

Raysa pulled another chair up and sat in front him, knee to knee. Her face reflected the horror he felt. "Surely not!"

"Lorena had me finish the autopsy because she was afraid the fumes from the alcohol might hurt her baby."

"The fumes were that strong?" Raysa leaned back in her chair and folded her arms across her ample bosom as if shielding herself from the truth. "But how … or *why* would Sister Susanna be drinking moonshine? Where did she get it? And why did it kill her?"

Huey, slightly revived from the strong drink, put down his glass and grabbed Raysa's trembling fists. "Princess, don't you go getting all upset about this, too. The Sheriff and Lorena will get this all sorted out. All I know is Susanna drank some pretty potent stuff. What the old timers call High Test Shine, doctored with Isopropanol, rubbing alcohol. It hit her pretty hard. She was in a coma before she even got to the tree that she smashed into."

Raysa gasped. "Good Lord!"

"Princess? Any more patients out there?" He motioned with a tilt of his head toward the waiting room.

"No. Miss Clarissa came in, complaining about her sore knees, but I gave her some pain rub and she left twenty minutes ago."

"Poor woman, ninety years old if she is a day, and her son Travis wants her to have a knee replacement." Doc shook his head. "With her brittle bones, a knee operation would break her tibia for sure. And then what?"

Raysa answered. "Then Travis and Cheri-Ann would have an excuse to park her in a nursing home."

"Not on my watch!" Doc snorted.

"Mine either."

They grinned at each other for a moment, partners in the important work of keeping the old timers, the Old Guard as Lorena called them, from being mistreated by their younger kin. Most of their medical practice consisted of the older members of Oakhill. The younger crowd drove up to the city and overpaid for their visits to the new breed of doctors whose specialities usually consisted of unnecessary procedures and cosmetic surgeries. Doc and Raysa knew the two of them were a dying breed of honest, tell it like it is, no nonsense, family doctors.

Now Raysa stared at the aging doctor. "I don't like the paleness of your skin, Doc. Makes me afraid for your health. You're not getting any younger, you know."

She leaned close to give him a big kiss on his forehead.

"And what would I do, what would any of us do, without you? I don't even want to think about a world without my beloved Huey."

She stood up abruptly and urged Doc to join her.

"Come on, Doc. Time for a nap before supper. I'll cook, you rest."

Together they walked toward the back door of the clinic. Huey's ancient cottage waited just a few steps away. He smiled and patted her arm, entwined with his.

"Raysa, my princess, you are a treasure beyond compare."

Chapter 16

Mayree

When Royal came to comfort her about the missing rosary, Mayree tried not to flinch. It had been so long since her husband had touched her with kindness, she hardly knew how to react. Mayree did admit to herself, grudgingly, that it actually felt good to be hugged again. She leaned her head against his narrow chest and tried not to sob. Royal hated it when she wept. She swiped away her tears with an always handy tissue and leaned back to study his face.

"So Susanna took Amilee's rosary? You know this for sure?"

Mayree nodded. "Grabbed it up and refused to give it back."

His expression hardened into deep rage. "She had no right to take anything of Amilee's, nun or no nun. I'm sorry, Sweetheart, but your sister was no saint, and I hate the very thought of her bringing you more grief and sorrow."

Sweetheart. Royal called me Sweetheart. Haven't heard that endearment in months.

Mayree gave her husband another long hug.

"I believe she took more than just Ami's rosary. I had that old collection of rosaries hidden in my jewelry box, you know, Mama's beads from when she was a child? Well, they're gone too."

Royal swore. He shrugged away from their shared hug and shook his fist at the ceiling.

"That meddlesome woman. I am glad she is dead!"

Mayree stared at the floor. *Me too,* she thought. But she felt it best not to say it out loud. Royal, after all, was the District Attorney. Best not to raise suspicion in his eyes.

"Did that Deputy find any rosaries in the car?" she asked.

"Keith? He didn't say anything about that when we were at McGee's Mortuary."

Royal heaved a big sigh and studied his wife's face for long moments.

"Best not say anything about this to Mother Superior this evening. She is staying for supper, I believe?"

Mayree nodded grimly. "And overnight too. I tell you Royal, it will feel good to have the house to ourselves again once we get shut of all those 'holy women'."

"Amen to that, Mayree. Amen to that."

Chapter 17

The Sheriff

After a phone call from Lorena, Lance called in Keith, his newly appointed deputy. *The kid tries hard, but he doesn't have enough experience yet to do a thorough investigation of a fatal accident.*

Keith stood before his boss as Lance stared down at him. Actually, they were both the same size, tall and burly, but when Lance stood behind his Sheriff's desk and glared, he felt taller than the younger man.

"So tell me again what you found at the accident scene early Tuesday morning."

Lance folded his arms across his chest and tapped the toe of one long cowboy boot. His posture shouted disapproval, but Keith did not waver or cower before his boss.

"I went to the scene of the accident, found the body of Sister Susanna pretty well tore up and bloody. She was pinned against the steering wheel and the seat. Took the 'jaws of life' to cut her body out for the ambulance crew to fuss over. Everybody could tell right away she was dead. No one could live through a crash like that."

Lance tapped his foot again. "And then what?"

For the first time, Keith's face looked troubled.

"So, I told the ambulance guys to take the body to Lorena's autopsy room, just like you told me to do."

The boot tapped again. Lance unfolded his arms and leaned across his scarred desk. The way Keith stared at those deep cuts and slashes in the Sheriff's desk, Lance figured his deputy wondered if they were from unlucky suspects being dragged across its surface. *Damn straight!* Lance thought.

"So did you search the car? Check for skid marks on the road? Look for signs of foul play on the body?"

"What do you mean, foul play?"

Lance sighed long and deep.

"Did you happen to notice whether either of her legs looked broken, pushed out of their hip sockets? Were there cuts on her forearms, signs of her shielding her face from the flying glass as she hit the tree?"

Keith looked bewildered. He shook his head.

"I just assumed she was driving drunk and hit the tree. She smelled pretty strong of booze when I found her."

Lance sighed again and reached for his Stetson.

"Come on, Kid. We're going back to the accident scene. You have a lot to learn about conducting a proper crime scene investigation."

Lance took his Harley. Keith drove his sedan and found himself breaking the local speed limit to stay within sight of the Sheriff's antique motorcycle. By noon they had a much longer and more detailed report to hand to Royal Taylor, the D.A.

Chapter 18

Royal

Lance and Keith sat in chairs across the desk from the District Attorney, Royal Taylor. One glance at their troubled faces and Royal knew the report in front of him could not be good news. He flicked at the edges of the papers before reading a single word.

"So, gentlemen, what is your opinion regarding the death of my wife's sister, Susanna?"

"Looks like foul play to me, Royal," Lance rumbled. "I know this is a delicate situation, Susanna being a nun and your wife's sister, but there will have to be an inquest. Somebody has to be held responsible for Sister Susanna's untimely demise. And we plan to discover who and what caused her death."

Royal leaned forward, bewildered. "Foul play? Really?"

Keith's dark eyes flickered uneasily as he glanced toward the Sheriff. Lance cleared his throat, then leaned forward without saying a word.

Neither man wished to speak, apparently. Royal tapped the closed report again.

"So what is in here that has the two of you so tongue-tied? Lance, you never seemed to be at a loss for words before."

The Sheriff sighed and sat back without opening his trap.

"Come, come, both of you! I realize my sister-in-law was not a saint! Believe me, Mayree and I ... Well let's just say that nun made herself pretty unwelcome in our so-called happy home. So whatever

49

is in this report that makes you so close-mouthed, just say it and be done with it."

He leaned back and waited, arms folded.

Finally Keith spoke up.

"Mr. Taylor, the Sheriff and I found a lot of puzzling information while investigating this death."

He hesitated, glanced at Lance's mulish face, then continued.

"For one thing, Sister Susanna was highly intoxicated before she drove into that tree."

Royal sat forward. His blue eyes widened with astonishment.

"Susanna drank? I never noticed her even taking a *sip* of liquor in my house."

Lance spoke up. "Not only did she drink, but she over-dosed on moonshine. Doc Huey said it was high-test shine, laced with rubbing alcohol."

"What? I can't believe this."

Royal sank back against the soft cushion of his office chair.

"Overdosed, Doc said?"

Lance's voice rumbled, breaking the shocked silence.

"Royal, the nun was out before she even hit the tree. No tire tracks. No defensive cuts on her arms like there would be if she tried to shield her face. Neither of her legs were broken or forced out of their hip sockets. Usually in an accident like this, the driver would see the tree coming and brace herself before impact. She was unconscious, probably in a coma, before she smacked up against that tree."

"Are you sure she was drinking? Maybe she had a stroke or something?"

Keith glanced down as if he read something too painful on Royal's face.

"Sir, the first thing I noticed when I got to the accident scene was the strong smell of alcohol coming from the body."

Royal stared at the two men for long moments. His gut churned and threatened to disgrace him in a violent spray of vomit. He swallowed several times, unable to speak.

Mayree will go ballistic when she hears this. Susanna, drinking shine? Impossible!

"Any other bad news for me today, gentlemen?"

His voice sounded raw as if he had spewed forth his breakfast coffee after all.

Lance said, "Just one more thing. We found this gold flask flattened between the dashboard and the front seat of her car."

He fished out the flask hidden deeply in the thick leather of his coat pocket.

"Did you ever see it before, Royal?"

Gut won out over propriety. Royal leaped up from his chair and raced to his private bathroom. Even through the closed solid oak door, Lance and Keith heard the District Attorney violently heaving up his breakfast.

Chapter 19

Lorena

Lorena, sitting in her home office, leaned over her desk as she reviewed Doc's notes about the autopsy of Sister Susanna. She clucked softly at the evidence of alcohol poisoning in the body of the "holy woman."

Nearby, at his own desk, Stuart Bouton interrupted his work as he poured over the financial ledger for the mortuary. His nearly bald head snapped up as he glanced at Lorena. His bushy eyebrows scowled with alarm.

"Something amiss, Lorena?"

She waved away his concern.

"Nothing financial, Stu," she said and hid a smile.

Anything to do with money, or the possible misuse of it, raised the hackles of her brother-in-law who also worked as her bookkeeper. It was family legend, Stuart's alarm about anything concerning money or the misuse of it. *He can't help it,* she thought. His money fears were triggered by the uncontrollable spending habits of his wife, Blanche. If Lorena hadn't hired Stuart last year to monitor her business accounts, and paid him a generous salary, the Bouton's might be bankrupt by now.

Stuart leaned back, making his office chair squeak.

"So why the big scowl, Lorena? Something rotten in Oakhill about Susanna's death?"

Lorena heaved a long sigh.

She pushed herself away from the desk and began to pace around the office.

"You know about how I had to leave the autopsy room?"

He nodded. "I thought it might be morning sickness or something."

She smiled wryly. *No secrets in this family,* she thought.

"Actually, Stuart, the body on the table had a strong odor of alcohol, especially after I made the first incision. Doc recognized, from the amount of damage to Susanna's trachea and bronchial tubes, that the quantity of blood was from that 'holy woman' drinking moonshine."

"Moonshine?" Stuart's jaw dropped in astonishment

"Yes, Huey called it high test shine, salted with rubbing alcohol. Isopropanol is the medical term for it."

"Impossible to believe!"

"Yeah, me too. When I leaned over to take a sniff, Doc pulled me away from the table and ordered me out of the room."

"Good thing he did, Lorena. You don't want anything to hurt that precious baby."

"My thoughts exactly. Thanks Stuart. You are a family prize for certain."

Stuart flushed. He did not receive many complements at home, she truly believed. Blanche could be a sweet soul, but when it came to appreciating her hard working husband, she often poo-pooed his good intentions with a wave of her hand accompanied by the jingling of her ever present jewelry.

"Ah, Lorena. Could I ask you something? I need some good advice about …"

"Of course. How can I help you? Is it Blanche spending too much again? Do you need a raise in salary here?"

He shook his head. "No, you have been more than generous to me, Lorena. This is something else." He bit his lips until his mustache almost disappeared.

She smiled to encourage him, sat down at her desk, and waited for him to work up enough nerve to ask whatever it was that had him so tongue tied.

"It's just that Monsignor McGaffee asked me to audit the church books. He called this morning before you came down."

"Wasn't that what Susanna was doing for him, too? Before she died, I mean."

He nodded. "Something about the collections being off, cash-wise, Father said."

Her eyebrows drew together. She drummed her fingers on the desk.

"Hmmm. Money problems at the church, and now Sister Susanna died in a suspicious accident? Could this be connected somehow?"

Stuart shrugged and spread his hands.

"Anything is possible, Lorena."

They stared at each other for long silent moments. Finally Stuart spoke again.

"So, do you mind if I take a look at the ledgers at St. Peter and Paul church?"

"Of course not, Stu. I want to get to the bottom of this mystery, too."

She grinned slightly. "Is the old tightwad going to pay you for your work?"

"Father did mention a small 'finder's fee.'"

"Don't let him low-ball you, Stuart. You are worth every penny I pay you and more. Ask for a regular hourly wage and stick to it. No salary, no work, period."

"Thanks, Lorena. Means a lot to be appreciated."

He hesitated, then plunged in to the most difficult part of the conversation.

"Ah, Lorena. I would consider it a personal favor if you keep this between you and me. If Blanche finds out I am working a second job, her spending will just escalate. You know how she is about tossing money around."

Lorena grinned. "This is our secret, Stuart. Good luck to you!"

She stood up and approached his desk.

"And by the way, please don't mention anything about the autopsy results. To *anyone*! You know how rumors spread around here. We do need a fighting chance to catch whomever killed that nun."

He nodded sagely. "Yes, indeed. My lips are sealed. You can count on me."

She leaned over his desk and gave him a big hug. It rocked him back in his chair in total surprise. As usual, when surprised by anything, his nose began to drip. He reached for a tissue and swiped it away.

"Hmmm, I think I like this new Lorena. My new boss, Mrs. Lundrum."

"Let's just keep it Lorena, for now OK, Stu? I'll claim the Mrs. title when I become a mama again."

Chapter 20

Monsignor Sean McGaffee

Monsignor hovered over Stuart's shoulder as his newly hired accountant paged through the parish financial ledger. Stuart seemed to shrink away every time Sean leaned closer to peer at the numbers on the yellow pages. The pastor finally noticed that his ever-looming presence served as a deterrent to Mr. Bouton's concentration. He took a step back and heaved a long sigh.

"I'm sorry, Stuart. Numbers have always been somewhat of a mystery to me. Can you make sense of any of this?"

He gestured toward the ledger, marred by numerous scribbled notes from Susanna's audit.

"Well, Father. I am getting a sense of what Sister meant by her notes. But it will take some time to go over all the accounts before I find the true picture of what she found in here."

He tapped the scribbling on the open page in front of him.

"It's Monsignor, not Father," Sean began in a droning huff. He dearly loved being addressed by his full title, rather than by the generic *Father*. Yet his new auditor was not of the Faith, so why did it matter what he called him? Sean sighed.

"I'm sorry, Mr. Bouton. Sometimes my pride gets the better of my good sense. You were saying?"

Stuart sniffed and reached for a tissue. His nose always picked the worse time to betray him by running whenever he felt threatened in any way. The hovering priest, this *Monsignor*, brought out all the insecurities that fed his dratted runny nose.

"Father, er Monsignor, your nun must have found something in here that isn't quite kosher. She might have discovered whose hand might be dipping into your till, so to speak."

Sean patted his pockets until he found the note Susanna had left him. Her last message before she died. The priest's wrinkled hand trembled as he handed the note to Stuart.

"I sincerely pray that this did not get Sister killed," he said. His voice shook.

Stuart read the scribbled note. *Sean, I believe I found our thief. Talk to you tomorrow.* His eyes widened as he stared up at Monsignor.

"You think someone might have murdered her? Sister Susanna, a holy nun?"

A knock on the office door interrupted them.

"Father? It's lunch time. Shall I set another plate for your friend?"

Monsignor glanced at Stuart.

"Hungry? Mrs. T makes a wonderful chef salad."

Stuart sniffed, blotting his nose. He nodded, reluctant to leave the paper work. But he had skipped breakfast. Just the mention of food and his stomach growled long and loud.

"Thank you for the invitation. I would certainly appreciate a nice healthy salad."

The pastor grinned. His stomach was talking to him, too. He shouted over his shoulder.

"Sure Kat, we'll be finished here in a few moments."

Stuart's eyes widened at the shouted order. But Sean shrugged and spread his hands.

"My housekeeper is 'slightly' deaf." He made quote marks with his fingers over the *slightly* part of his speech. "She is a dear woman, a bit bossy, a tiny bit nosy, but faithful to the core. You will enjoy her meal, believe me, Mr. Bouton."

"Just call me Stu. Everybody does."

"And I am Sean to my friends."

The men shook hands and left the office. Sean closed and locked the door behind him.

It made Stuart wonder just how faithful or how trustworthy the pastor believed his housekeeper to be, really, if he locked his private office from the prying nose of his "dear woman."

A third person joined the lunch crowd, Ned Turnipseed. Stuart remembered him from childhood. *Seedy* the school kids called him since his white-blond hair stuck up resembling an oversized dandelion gone to seed. The men spread napkins on their laps. Sean led the blessing, thanking God for the food and the fellowship. As Mrs. T served huge salads to each man, Stuart turned to Seedy.

"So how goes it with the Children's Saving Network, Mr. Turnipseed?"

"It's Deacon Ned now, Stuart. Finished my training last month. Took my vows just after Labor Day."

"Congratulations, Seedy, er Deacon Ned. Does that mean you are a priest now?"

Ned shook his head. "No, just limited privileges in the church. I can perform weddings, Baptisms, funerals, preach an occasional sermon, if Monsignor allows me to do it."

"Well, good for you."

Stuart smiled and extended his hand.

"But how is the CSN doing? Did you have to resign from that organization? Lorena says you did good work with those forgotten children. She called them, 'throw away children'. Is that the right term?"

Ned nodded as he forked up a big bite of meat-laden salad.

"Great meal, Ma'am."

The housekeeper beamed and patted his shoulder as she hustled around the table, pouring beverages. Ned chewed and swallowed before he answered Stuart's question.

"The Children's Saving Network is my life's mission. I hope to help as many hurt and abandoned children as I can. They are so needy! Some don't even have rosary beads! At meetings, we always begin by saying the rosary. It hurts my soul to see so many children using their fingers to count off the decades. It's shameful. Monsignor allowed me to put a special box in the back of the church, and parishioners have been donating rosaries for the cause."

Ned could have gone on preaching for hours, but Monsignor laid a firm hand on his arm.

"Let's just enjoy this wonderful meal, shall we gentlemen? Kat has worked all morning to provide this excellent repast."

He shot a quick smile to his housekeeper and gestured over the food.

"Besides, Mr. Bouton needs to go back to work on the accounts. Right Stu?"

The rest of the meal passed in a somewhat sullen silence. None of the men lifted their eyes from their plates, except to sip coffee or sweet tea. Mrs. T did not offer dessert.

Chapter 21

Belle

As Belle coaxed Lorena to eat something for lunch, her hands shook. Lorena glanced up, puzzled. Her housekeeper, the gem who lived with them and kept her handicapped son out of mischief, seemed distracted by something.

"Are you all right, Belle? Is something wrong?"

Belle dropped into the chair opposite Lorena and wrung her hands in her lap. Her face twisted as she struggled to express, in words, the complications of her problem.

"Well, Miss Lorena, it's just that …"

Lorena put down her fork and leaned across the table.

"Belle, you know you can trust me. I won't judge you no matter what happened. I am not like your former husband. No way!"

Words gushed out of Belle.

"It's just that sweet boy, Johnny. You know how he is, takes a liking to somebody and just won't quit trying to help out? In any way he can, or thinks he can."

Lorena sighed. "So what has John-Duncan been up to these days? Must be something important or you wouldn't be so upset. Don't worry, Belle, I know how bull-headed he can be when he makes up his mind about something. So, what now?"

"Johnny has taken a liking to that new ground's keeper, that nephew of mine, Zack. Follows him around, tries to help him mow grass in the cemetery or move the urns around."

Lorena folded her arms.

"Doesn't sound so bad. I know Zack keeps an eye out so John-Duncan doesn't get hurt. I watched him mow grass this morning. He does a good job, even with my son's 'help.'"

"Yes, but that's not all your boy's been doing. Yesterday, at noon time, he carried Zack up that long stairway to the kitchen, just so Zack could have lunch with us."

Lorena leaned back in her chair, astonished.

"I never realized my son was so strong. I know he's been piling on the pounds, and the muscle, since you came to cook for us. But lugging Zack up the stairway? Wow!"

She frowned at the implications. Across the table, Belle bit her lips.

"Even before he brought Zack up the steps, Johnny carried up that extra wheelchair you always keep in the viewing rooms. At least I think that's where he got it." Belle flushed. "You know how I am, Miss Lorena. Get the willies just thinking about what goes on downstairs in your funeral parlor."

Lorena smiled faintly. "I know, Belle. And don't feel alone. Plenty of people are afraid to enter my humble establishment, even when one of their loved ones is laid out in the viewing room. Makes me wonder if they think the corpse is going to rise up, point a bony finger, and accuse them of some wrong doing in the past!"

Belle shuddered.

"I know it just hain't so, Miss Lorena, but old fears are hard to get shut of, you know?"

Lorena nodded. "But this new problem, John-Duncan carrying Zack up those steps … Something has to change. It's not safe."

"He could get hurt. Both of them could go cartwheeling down those steps! It made my heart stop when I saw what they were up to, those two guys. They were laughing and joking the whole way up the steps. Zack was riding Johnny's back like he was on a bucking bronco. Don't worry, Miss Lorena. I reamed them out proper for pulling such a dangerous stunt. But you know how stubborn Johnny can be?"

"Oh, yes. I do know how John-Duncan can be, believe me. He's pulled some spectacular tantrums since he came home to live, but nothing like this."

The boy had spent the first eighteen years of his life in a home for special needs students. When he aged out of that system, Lorena brought him home to live with her. It caused a scandal at the time, a single woman suddenly and publicly the mother of an obviously handicapped son. Yet Lorena held her head high and ignored the gossip. Eventually, the dark rumors died down. Of course, it never affected her business. People stilled died and needed the attention of the only mortician in the area, Lorena McGee. Now she was also the Coroner of the county, so her services were even more vital to the families of deceased loved ones.

"What can we do, Miss Lorena?"

Lorena smiled and reached for her cell phone.

"Now, Belle, we call someone to install a chair lift so Zack can ride up in style whenever he wants to come for lunch."

Belle looked stricken. "Won't something like that cost the earth?"

Lorena grinned. "Stuart has been campaigning for a chair lift ever since we hired Zack. He says the cost of it can be deducted as a business expense on our taxes. It's a win-win situation, or so Stu claims. And he does know his numbers, right?"

Belle jumped up and gave Lorena a long hug.

"Oh Miss Lorena, you are the best. Thank you so much."

Lorena grinned. "And now maybe we can invite Zack's wife, Mavis and their daughter Lilly-Belle to supper, too. I've been dying to see that new little girl. Maybe Mavis will let me hold her? Been a long time since I held a newborn. Need some practice for the future, right?"

"You bet, Miss Lorena. I will invite them over whenever you say."

"How about tomorrow night?"

"Don't you have a funeral to do? Sister Susanna, that nun who died the other day?"

Lorena shook her head.

"No, the head of her convent, Mother Superior Ann Mary, escorted her body back to Biloxi as soon as Doc finished the autopsy. *Rules*, you know. Her funeral Mass will be celebrated at the convent this evening."

Chapter 22

Lorena and Lance

Lance returned to their apartment late that afternoon. He seemed extra thoughtful, his head hanging down studying his boots, as he climbed the long stairway. Lorena waited at the top of the steps. He looked up, forced a smile, and walked into her warm hug.

"Ah, just what I needed after a long stressful day: a hug from my sweetheart."

They swayed together for long moments. Lorena studied his gloomy expression.

"So what has my new husband so down in the dumps this fine autumn day?"

He heaved a long sigh and ran thick fingers through his bushy curls.

"Ah, Lorena, my love, this thing with that nun … It has me unsettled for sure."

"Because she drank alcohol before she crashed? Does that shake your fine sense of what is right and proper for a holy woman? Is that what has you so low down and blue?" she said, and grinned. "Sounds like a country/western song in the making, ya think?"

"Not funny, my dear. Not funny at all. Keith and I, plus Doc Huey, we all think Sister Susanna was deliberately murdered."

Lorena frowned. Her eyes tracked back and forth as she mentally reviewed the autopsy report. *High test moonshine, Doc said. Surely a nun, even one who secretly drank, would not deliberately risk her life by ingesting something so powerful, and so deadly. Especially before jumping into her car and trying to drive home.*

"I think you may be right, Lance. About Susanna being deliberately poisoned, I mean. But who would want her dead? And why, for heaven's sake, would a nun be the target of a murderer?"

Lance hooked his arm around Lorena's waist as they walked toward the kitchen.

"That, my dear, is what we aim to find out."

Chapter 23

Moving Night

That night after supper, Lorena shooed John-Duncan to his room to watch a video. The boy/man loved anything put out by Disney. Tonight's movie was a favorite: Cinderella. Even from the kitchen, the adults could hear the echo of the boy's singing as he mimicked the music score of the film. Belle interrupted her clean-up duties to check in on him every five minutes.

Lance and Lorena moved to the living room and sat together on the sofa. They cuddled briefly, enjoying their precious time alone, before Lorena got down to the business at hand. She explained the need for a chair lift for Zack and Lance agreed immediately to the idea. The next item up for discussion really caught his attention.

"What do you think about Zack, Mavis and their baby moving in here with us?"

"Why, Lorena? Don't we have enough live-in help now?"

Lorena patted his arm and leaned closer for a whispered conversation.

"I am thinking of moving out of our bedroom and into the suite down the hall. More privacy for us for our private moments, you understand?"

Lance's brown eyes lit up.

"You mean, more freedom to exercise our marital rights, without interruption?"

She nodded. Several times in the past few days, John-Duncan, awakened from his sleep by the joyful sounds on the other side of their shared wall, had knocked on their locked bedroom door.

"Mama! Are you OK? I heard yelling in there."

Lorena had been forced to untangle herself from her new husband's fierce embrace, then grab a robe, unlock the door, and reassure her son that indeed, everything was all right. Some nights it took quite a bit of persuasion to usher the overgrown boy back to his bed.

"So, if we move down the hall, then Zack and Mavis can move in? Is that what you're planning, my wicked little witch?"

He kissed her behind the ear sending chills down her spine.

"Not only that, Lance, but Belle really needs extra help with John-Duncan. She can't be everywhere at once, and my boy has been getting too darned independent these days."

"Yeah. John-Duncan's carrying Zack up the steps was just plain fool-hardy."

"Plus, that young couple will liven up the place. Just think, Lance, a baby in our house! It will give me practice for when our little one is born."

"Give us both practice, Lorena. You know I have been a bachelor all my life. Never found anyone I wanted to hitch up with until you came along and stole my heart." He grinned and nibbled on her ear again. "Babies are a whole 'nother world for me."

"Me too, Lance. You realize, of course, that I never had a chance to take care of John-Duncan when he was an infant?"

"Oh, how come?"

"If you recall, I was just fifteen when my baby boy was born. My grandmother Songier, down in Mississippi, delivered him herself. When I reached for him, she whisked him away with a big frown. 'Oh no, no, Lorena. Best you don't get attached to your precious son. You can't take the baby home with you. Your father, Duncan, put his foot down on that. And you don't want to raise this innocent babe in my house, do you?'"

Lorena frowned. "Grandma ran a 'house of ill repute' as they called it in those days. She housed a crowd of beautiful young women of every race and disposition. Each girl kept busy 'entertaining' the lustful men in that town. 'A necessary service to the community' Grandma claimed and smiled her famous welcoming grin."

Lorena sighed. "I could see her point about not subjecting John-Duncan to that lifestyle, but it killed my soul when she handed him over to the orphan home run by the Grey Nuns of the Sacred Heart."

"Don't cry, child," she kept telling me. "Your boy will be adopted by some loving couple and live a better life than any of us here."

"Only …"

"Only, what, Lorena?" But he already knew the answer.

"Only no one wanted to adopt a 'special needs' baby, no matter how handsome he was or how beautiful his loving smile. I used to visit him twice a month, whenever Duncan would drive me down for a day. But a day's worth of cuddling and kissing my boy never seemed enough. Finely, when he aged out of the system, they let me bring him home."

"I remember the occasion, Lorena. It was old Mrs. Wilton's funeral, right?"

He grinned and hugged her tight.

"My, how the gossips craned their necks that morning, remember?"

She laughed. "It didn't help any when he and Raysa began to sing the closing funeral hymn. In that too quiet church, their duet created a sensation!"

"Your boy can sing all right, Lorena."

She nodded agreement.

"But about the other matter, Zack's family moving in here. Are you all right with it?"

He chuckled. "Anything you want, Darlin'."

"Good. Thanks Lance. Zack's family is coming for supper tomorrow night. We can talk about it then. Sure hope they agree. I'm really looking forward to having a baby in the house."

"And I'm looking forward to our new bedroom arrangement."

Chapter 24

Royal

Royal, still pale from his bout of vomiting, sifted through the documents left by the Sheriff and his Deputy an hour before. They had taken the evidence bag, containing the flattened flask, with them. No matter. He knew at first glance the golden flask, now crushed and useless, had belonged to him. It was an heirloom, handed down from his great-great-grandfather. Family rumor said it had been one of the spoils of war, stolen from a Yankee Captain whose luck ran out during the battle for Atlanta during the War between the States.

My flask. And how or why did Sister Susanna end up with it?

He had not noticed it missing. Usually kept in the top drawer of his office desk, he no longer carried it to work each day. After the death of their daughter, his wife had been so out of control, downing sedatives like candy mints, then drinking so freely from his collection of bourbon, blended whiskey, and vodka, that it scared him. Scared Hannah too. She came to him one evening a few weeks ago, after Mayree passed out in her bedroom upstairs.

"Mmmmmister Ttttaylor," she began, struggling to control her speech.

Royal took pity on the poor tongue-tied woman. He placed a soothing arm around her waist and guided her to a nearby chair.

"Just take it slow, Hannah. We have all night to talk. Deep breaths, remember?"

Finally, Hannah settled down. The gist of her request was simple,

"Could you hide some of your liquor bottles, Sir? I'm afffffaid Miss May might overdose."

Royal frowned. He slowly nodded agreement.

"Thank you, Hannah. I've been trying not to notice how bad my wife is getting. This is a wake-up call for me. I'll lock up everything right now."

True to his word, Royal hid his collection of liquor in a locked cabinet and kept the key in his pocket. He also cut down on his own drinking. He needed all his wits about him to keep track of Mayree. His wife needed medical help for her depression, he realized.

"I'll call Doc Huey in the morning for a reference," he told his housekeeper.

Mayree now consulted a mental health specialist twice a week, in the privacy of their living room. Yet Royal distinctly remembered leaving the antique flask in the top drawer of his desk. *Did Mayree grab it up before she got help for her drinking, and spirit it away somewhere? A handy source for a quick nip when she felt overwhelmed with grief? But then, how did her sister, the nun, get her hands on it? And why was it found in her car, with traces of high-test moonshine in it?*

But what bothered Royal the most was the upcoming inquest into Sister Susanna's death. How could he possibly explain that the crushed flask actually belonged to him, the District Attorney of Colquitt County? *And where on earth did Susanna get moonshine in the first place?*

Chapter 25

Kathleen

Kathleen had not been sleeping well all week. As housekeeper for Monsignor Sean McGaffee, she felt responsible for maintaining a calm peaceful atmosphere in the rectory. Since the death of that meddling nun, *that Sister Susanna!,* nothing had been peaceful or calm in her private little kingdom. Why even the Sheriff that hillbilly Lance Lundrum, rider of motorcycles of all things, dared to disturb her busy day. That cycle roared so loud, it's a wonder the deceased loved ones in the cemetery failed to arise when the big galoot came stomping up to the front door. She took her time answering his pounding knock. Kat did not want to answer the door at all. She heaved a long sigh, obviously visible to Lance, as she reluctantly opened the door. She watched as the Sheriff swallowed back his anger and touched the brim of his wide-brimmed hat, a sign (barely) of respect. He bowed slightly.

"Mrs. T? Is the good Pastor in residence this morning?"

She sniffed as if his polite question gave off an offensive odor.

"Monsignor has a meeting with the Bishop today. He won't be back until dinner time."

The Sheriff's face darkened.

"Then you will have to do. I need some answers."

He took a step and loomed over her. She felt threatened by the sheer size of the man. Kat gasped, frightened by an obscure guilt thudding her heart. Mrs. T stepped back, her hand clasped to the

71

knob for support, and widened the opening of the door. The Sheriff stepped into the foyer and removed his Stetson.

"Thank you, Ma'am. Where can we talk?"

She motioned to the kitchen. He followed her through a large living room. The thick carpet, a deep forest green, made him smile.

"Nice rug, Mrs. T. It feels soft under these old feet."

I just wonder how much walking he does anyhow, she thought. *Those cowboy boots don't look very comfortable with their pointed toes and all.*

"Why don't you wear regular men's shoes instead of those old boots?" She spoke before she could stop herself. Flustered by her boldness, she continued. "I mean, pointed toes and all, that must make for painful walking, don't you think?"

His face, the skin usually a sun-browned tan resembling half-cured leather, turned a deeper red.

"Well, Mrs. T, it's tough to find any shoe large enough to fit my feet. Have to order these boots from Boot-Daddy, a company online. You know, on the internet?"

"Yes, Ned has a computer in his office here. He tried to show me how to use it, but I don't have time for all that modern foolishness. Just keeping the rectory clean and Monsignor fed, keeps me busy enough these days."

She motioned to Lance where to sit at the table, and settled into a chair across from him. She tried to keep her voice steady as the Sheriff began his questions.

"Now, Mrs. T, from all accounts, you are the last person to see Sister Susanna before she died. Am I right on that?"

She bit her lips and nodded. His face reflected frustration as he waited for an answer, a comment, a thought, *something* to clear up the mystery surrounding the nun's sudden death. Kat remained silent. The Sheriff drummed his thick fingers on the table top. She felt mild surprise when they didn't leave dents in the smooth surface. The man was *big!*

Lance leaned back in his chair. It squeaked a protest at his weight.

"Now Ma'am, surely you can tell me something about that day. Supper time, right? What did Susanna say to you. Anything at all?"

Kat tightened her lips, remembering the way Sister Susanna shouted at her all the way from the main office. *Like I was a runaway dog or something!* She cleared her throat.

"Sister lost track of her purse. She yelled at me as if I were a common thief with nothing better to do than sneak around stealing purses, for the love of God!"

Lance's eyes grew so wide, new wrinkles appeared. He drew a deep breath. Kat could almost read the thoughts racing behind those deep brown eyes. *Suspicious thoughts!*

"So, she yelled at you? Then what?"

It took her a few deep breaths to compose herself. She folded her hands in her lap to stop their trembling.

"Then she came storming in here, into the kitchen. I pointed out her purse, where she dumped it on the counter when she came in that morning. Told her I never touched it. Such a suspicious person, that meddling nun! Wonder what she had hidden in there that made her so uppity when she couldn't find it?"

Lance's fingers were drumming again. He heaved a long sigh and stared out the window. Rows of white headstones marched across an immaculate lawn. Made him shiver a bit.

"I hate cemeteries. Too much sadness. Too many good people gone from this tired old earth. Makes me feel lonesome for my loved ones gone on before."

Kat surprised herself. She reached across the table and patted his restless fingers.

"You are not alone in that thought, Sheriff."

He shook off his dark thoughts and tried to smile.

"Back to business," he said. "So what happened next? Did Sister stay for supper?"

His tone seemed softer for that brief moment of sympathy shared between them. Kat response seemed softer too.

"No, she used the facilities. The door is behind you, Sheriff, if you need them."

He shook his head and flushed.

"I asked her to stay for supper, but she complained of a bad headache. No wonder she had a headache if you ask me! She skipped dinner that day, just kept working away in Monsignor's office. A sensible person knows a body can't go without food without coming down with a headache. A migraine, she called it. She grabbed up her purse and hustled out of here. I heard the tires squealing as she left the parking lot. Not the first time, believe me. Sister had a lead foot when it came to driving. It's a wonder that old car of her's had any tread left on the tires at all."

Lance frowned and stood up.

"One more question, then I need to meet with the D.A. again. Was there anyone else here in the rectory last Monday, besides you and Susanna, I mean?"

Kat glanced down at her clenched fists. Instinct made her shield her grandson from suspicion. He had been so upset when he moped into her kitchen that morning. *Looked like his world had just fallen apart, he did*, she thought. Kat stiffened her shoulders and stared right at Lance as she lied to his face.

"No, Sheriff. Just Monsignor, and he left right after breakfast for sick calls. He was gone all afternoon."

Lance did not look happy as he walked out the front door. Moments later, she heard his motorcycle roar out of the parking lot. *More black marks on the pavement*, she mused. She let out the long breath she had been holding. Dark spots danced before her eyes. She felt giddy with relief.

Chapter 26

Raysa

Lorena sat on the doctor's exam table, clutching a paper gown under her folded arms. Raysa pried one arm loose to take her patient's blood pressure.

"So, how are you feeling these days, Lorena?" Raysa asked as she pumped up the blood pressure cuff.

"Sleepy all the time!" Lorena said and grinned. "Hungry too. This baby is going to be a giant according to how often he demands food!" She patted the baby mound. "He must be growing like a wild weed. I don't remember being this big at four months when I was pregnant with John-Duncan."

Raysa smiled. "Every pregnancy is different, Lorena. Besides, look at the baby's daddy. Lance is pretty big himself, you know."

Lorena grinned. "Big in, big out. Is that what you're saying?" She blushed.

Raysa laughed and nodded. She paused, listening to the sounds from the stethoscope buds in her ears.

"Good pressure, Lorena. Keep up the good work. Some mother's are plagued with sky-high blood pressure and it's so dangerous for the unborn babe."

Lorena said, "I try to stay calm. Not always easy with John-Duncan around."

"What has my favorite nephew been up to this time?"

Lorena rolled her eyes. "His latest trick is carrying 'my friend Zack' up that long back stairway. Belle almost had a conniption fit when she caught them staggering up the steps, laughing and joking like a couple of collage roommates coming home from a night on the town." Lorena sighed. "I ordered a stair lift as soon as I heard about it. Stuart had been after me about it for weeks it seems. But with all the wedding plans…" She shrugged and spread her hands.

Raysa patted her shoulder. "You can't remember everything, Lorena. Right now your main job is taking care of yourself and Junior here." She patted Lorena's abdomen.

"I know your adult son is a big challenge for you. All that strength and energy, and little real sense of danger. A teenager in a man's body."

Raysa unwrapped a stick of cinnamon gum and folded it into her mouth as she thought of solutions for her friend.

"How about I send Rocket Man over for a little dog and boy exercise? I know my dog needs a workout to calm him down these days. I spend a lot of time here with Doc, and Rocket Man gets pretty lonely shut up in that big house we live in. Every night I come home, a new surprise! The other day he dragged a stray ground squirrel through the doggy dog. They were having a good game of chase when I walked in. Never saw a squirrel so happy to escape!" She laughed at the memory.

Lorena grinned. "They do much damage to your house?"

"Just a lot of skid marks on the floor, couple of gee-gaws broken. Nothing I cared about anyway." She frowned. "Thing is, I worry about Doc these days. He isn't getting any younger. That's why I spend so much time here with him in the evenings."

Lorena patted her arm. "Send your dog to visit anytime. John-Duncan has been pestering me for a dog ever since Amilee's funeral when your brought Rocket to visit that evening."

"Thanks Lorena."

The women were hugging as Doc walked into the exam room.

Chapter 27

Suppertime

Lorena gazed around the kitchen table crowded with happy people. Zack, in his wheelchair, sat at one end of the oblong table, Lance faced him from the other end. Lorena sat to the left of her husband with Mavis, holding her baby girl, sharing their side of the table. John-Duncan and Belle filled the opposite side. Zack led the blessing.

"O Loving Father, we thank Thee for the blessings of food and fellowship. In Jesus' name we pray."

"Amens" echoed around the table.

Everyone smiled, happy to be together, grateful to be sharing Belle's excellent fried chicken with all the trimmings. Knives and forks clicked as the group dug into the excellent down home meal. John-Duncan picked up a drumstick and chomped down a huge bite.

"Johnny, remember, use your fork," Belle said and poked the boy with her elbow.

His dark blue eyes rolled as he gulped down the oversized bite of chicken.

"But, Grandma Belle ..." he began.

Lorena cleared her throat and gave her son a long glare. He dropped the drumstick and swiped at his face with his napkin.

"Sorry," he said. Reluctantly, he picked up knife and fork and attacked the chicken on his plate. "It just smelled so good, I couldn't wait for a bite."

Lance chuckled. "Know that feeling, Son. But manners are important, too."

Outnumbered, John-Duncan slid a pleading glance at his new best friend.

"Zack?" the boy whined, hoping for an encouraging word.

Zack shrugged and waved his tableware. "See, Johnny? Even people with no legs need to remember good table manners."

Mavis laughed. It served to break the mild tension at table.

"Don't fret, John-Duncan. It took me a while to teach this big hunk table manners, too."

Everyone thoroughly enjoyed the meal. As Belle began to clear the table, Mavis handed her infant to Lorena.

"Mind holding Lilly?" she said. "I want to help Aunt Belle."

Lorena gulped and opened her arms. She gazed down at the precious baby, just waking up from a nap. The infant stretched and yawned.

"Such a sweet gift from God," Lorena said. Her voice trembled. She hugged the baby and softly kissed the fussy down on her tiny head.

Lance looked on, his eyes shining. They were so taken up with the baby, neither Lance nor Lorena noticed when plates of fresh apple pie landed on the table before them. Mavis sat down and opened her arms for her baby. Lorena gave the infant back with obvious reluctance.

Lance cleared his throat. He gripped Lorena's hand and stared across the table at Zack.

"My wife and I have a proposition to offer you two. Well, actually you three."

"Oh?"

Both Zack and Mavis turned toward Lance. Lorena spoke up.

"We would like you, your little family that is, to move in here with us."

John-Duncan clapped his hands.

"Yay! Zack living here with us!"

The young couple looked astonished.

"But why?" Mavis said.

Lance took over. "For one thing, Zack, it means another man in the house, to help out so to speak. With my job and all, and Lorena's occupation keeping her so busy, it would ease our minds to know Belle had extra help keeping the peace around here."

They all glanced at John-Duncan, but no one made a comment about the boy/man with an adolescent's tendency toward mischief.

Mavis stared around the large room.

"Are you sure there is room enough here for another three people?"

The baby began to cry, a loud winding up to a full *I'm hungry* howl. Mavis jiggled the infant and lifted Lilly to her shoulder. She swayed back and forth, but the howls grew louder.

"That's another thing, Lance and Lorena." Zack said. "Can you stand hearing a baby cry like that? At all hours of the day and night? It can be hectic, I know, even with Mavis doing most of the baby care work."

Lorena smiled. "We'd better get used to it."

Lance grinned. "Yep, five months from now, we'll be jiggling a baby too."

Mavis shared a huge smile. "I had heard some rumors, but I wasn't sure ..."

"Congratulations, you two," Zack said.

"Thanks. We appreciate that. Just so you know, Mavis, this offer comes with a salary for you too."

"Really? For what? Just hanging around helping Aunt Belle? I would do that for nothing."

Lorena laid her hand on Mavis's shoulder.

"I need someone to teach me how to be a mom," she said softly. "I never had a chance to mother John-Duncan after his birth."

Mavis reached across the wailing infant and gave Lorena an awkward hug.

"You bet, I can help you, but I have a feeling you don't need much teaching, Lorena. You seem like a natural-born mothering type to me."

Lance glanced across the table. "You on board with all this, Zack?"

Zack leaned back in his wheelchair and swiped off his forehead. He grinned.

"Actually, this is a blessing to us. Our old trailer is falling apart but we couldn't even afford to look for a place to rent, let alone buy anything new. Since Harlan Parnell closed his mill and put Mavis out of a job, we have been squeaking along on my government disability check."

He shook his head. "Never again will I look down on those poor people on food stamps. We had to apply for W.I.C. last month, just to buy baby food for Lilly-Belle."

The housekeeper gasped. "If I had known how bad it was, I would have helped out."

"Now, Aunt Belle. You know how proud all the Jake family is. Rather starve than ask for help. Took a lot of pride swallowing before we applied for food stamps."

Mavis sighed as she cuddled the baby. When she glanced up, tears glittered in her eyes.

"Thank you all for asking us to move in with you. I know it is not charity, because nobody knew just how tough it was with us. Zack is right, this is a blessing. And I thank you both and God for giving us this chance to get back on our feet."

John-Duncan jumped up, dancing around the table, unable to control his joy. His hands clapped over and over again.

"Zack is coming. Zack is coming." Suddenly remembering his *manners*, he added, "And Mavis and the baby too. They are all coming. Hooray!"

Later, as Lance and Keith helped move a crib plus clothing and personal items into what had been Lorena's bedroom, John-Duncan kept dancing back and forth, unable to contain his joy.

Lorena took her son aside, sat him down, and waited until he calmed down a bit. She clutched his waving hands until they stilled. Leaning forward, she stared into his deep blue eyes.

"Now, Son, remember there will be some new rules for you to learn. And obey."

"Zack is coming!"

"I know, John-Duncan. But new people in the house means new *rules*, you understand?"

"Like what?"

His voice sounded pouty and sullen, a typical teenager's reaction to rules of any type. Lorena leaned closer to reinforce this important lesson.

"Like bedtime rules. Once Zack and Mavis go into their bedroom at night and shut the door, it means you do not bother them in any way. Not until morning."

John-Duncan looked confused. "Are they sleeping in your bed, Mama?"

She nodded.

"But I used to go into your room all the time at night."

"New rules, remember? I know it's hard to understand, but when a man and wife are married, they want *privacy* at night."

"Privacy?" he frowned briefly, then grinned slyly.

"Privacy like you and the Sheriff want now, too?"

"Yep. Same thing. Married people need privacy at night. Got it?"

His head hung down. He stared at his hands, quiet now since mama held them together so tightly. He nodded.

"But what if I have a bad dream, like I did one time. Can I go into your bedroom then?"

Lorena leaned back, releasing her grip on his hands.

"John, that was a year ago. You are a big boy now, a man, like Zack. You don't need your mama to comfort you if you have a bad dream. You just roll over and go back to sleep."

He straightened with pride. "I am a big man now, Mama. Like Zack, only with legs."

She gave him a long hug. "Yes, you are a big man like Zack. But please don't make him feel bad because he lost his legs in the war."

"I'm taller than Zack, Mama, because he has no legs."

"I know, son. Just don't hurt Zack's feelings, OK? Friends don't say hurtful things to other friends."

"I knoooow!" he said, so much like a teenager, Lorena had to laugh.

"Just remember, new *rules* for the bedrooms at night."

Lorena went to check on the new little family in her former bedroom. Everything fit in nicely, even all the baby equipment, the crib and the changing table. Mavis stood with an armful of little clothing staring around at the large dressers that lined one wall of Lorena's old bedroom.

"Don't hesitate to use the dresser space, Mavis," she said. "Belle and I cleaned out my stuff this afternoon, before you guys came for supper."

Mavis grinned. "Guess you were really counting on our moving in, I take it?"

Lorena hugged her and laughed. "We had high hopes."

Zack spoke up from the doorway. "I did notice you had a trapeze installed over the bed. Thanks, that will really help me get in and out of bed without my wife having to lift me. I swear she strained her back more than once. Even half a man is too heavy for a little gal like Mavis to wrestle onto the bed."

"I never minded helping you, Zack."

He moved closer and gave his wife a warm hug.

"I know, Sweetheart. But I minded. Sometimes I actually heard your spine crack!"

"Now you can swing into bed." John-Duncan said, dancing around the room. "Lucky you, Zack! Mama, can I have a swing in my room, too?"

It took another long conversation before John-Duncan calmed down and accepted that, no, he would not be swinging into bed, like *lucky Zack,* anytime soon.

Chapter 28

Royal

Royal Taylor mulled over the strange disappearance of his flask. His mind, sharpened by years as the District Attorney of Colquett County, who prosecuted criminals for both minor and major acts of disobedience to the criminal codes of Georgia, fretted as he read, yet again, the notes written by Doc Huey.

Principal cause of death caused by a lethal ingestion of Isopropanol, commonly sold as rubbing alcohol. Victim apparently unconscious or in a drug induced coma before her car hit the tree. Gold colored flask found in wreckage with residue of moonshine inside. No skid marks at the scene of accident tend to support this thesis. The victim was not conscious before she drove into the tree. Autopsy revealed massive hemorrhaging in throat, stomach and lungs.

Doc added a footnote in his typical scribble, "Not an easy way to die. Poor woman."

Royal slammed shut the folder and scowled. He leaned his elbows on the desk, folded his hands under his chin, and stared into space.

The flask. That dratted flask! How did she get her hands on it? Did someone here at the house give it to Susanna? Did she steal it from my desk?

His mind whirled like an endless toy exercise wheel, around and around, with no answers. At least none he wanted to contemplate at the moment.

"Moonshine!" he muttered aloud. "Where in the living hell did that nun pick up moonshine? *High test* moonshine, Doc said."

Hannah, listening at the closed door, leaped back as she heard Royal slam his fist against the desk. She scurried away, her slippers flapping as she escaped his wrath. Moments later Royal jerked open the thick door and bellowed loud enough so even Mayree, under the thundering shower, could hear the echo of his outrage.

"Somebody in this house knows something!" he shouted. "And I aim to find out just what happened here before Sister Susanna was murdered."

Chapter 29

Lorena

Royal's shouting could be heard through the front door as Lorena knocked. She hesitated, waiting for the tantrum to ease off, before she knocked again. Moments later, Royal jerked open the front door. He looked ready to smite someone, anyone, who dared to intrude on his private territory. His face fell as he recognized Lorena. The anger wrinkles quickly smoothed over as he bowed her into the foyer.

"Sorry, Lorena. Bad morning. Hannah should have let you in. I don't even know where she is. Must have scared her off, my shouting, that is. She sure is spooky these days. The least little thing, she jumps and disappears."

He sighed and ran thin fingers through his thick mane of blond hair. He deep blue eyes looked wary, troubled.

"Come in, Lorena. Didn't mean to bother you with my household problems. Want to sit in my office?"

He gestured toward the opened door to their left. Lorena nodded and led him into his home office. She sank into a chair near his desk, glanced briefly at the folder on its dark top, and heaved a long sigh.

"This nun thing sure has everyone upset," she said.

"Tell me about it," he said, not a question, but a wry observation.

Lorena leaned across the desk, shoving the folder aside as she stared up into her boss's face.

"But Susanna's death is not why I am here. You can work all that out with the Sheriff and Deputy Keith."

She paused, gathering strength for her big announcement.

"Royal, I am here to resign my position as Coroner of Colquitt County."

He dropped into his chair. His face betrayed complete bewilderment.

"But why? You are perfect for the job. What with all your experience as a mortician, your medical training ... Why are you quitting on me now?"

His voice sounded whiny like a child denied a favorite toy. He squirmed in the chair until the thick leather complained.

"You want to just up and quit now, when I need that fine brain power of yours to help me solve this murder case? Did I do something to offend you just when I need you so much, Lorena?"

Lorena smiled and hugged her growing belly.

"No boss, nothing you did affected my decision." She patted her stomach. "In case you haven't noticed, I am pregnant."

He nodded, still puzzled. "You still haven't answered my question, Lorena. Being in the family way shouldn't have any bearing on your job as Coroner."

"But it does, Royal. During Susanna's autopsy, I leaned over to take a whiff of that strong alcohol smell in her incision, and Doc had a fit. He grabbed me before I even got close to the body and dragged me halfway across the room." She grimaced at the memory. "Huey told me that even inhaling that Isopropanol could singe my lungs and even hurt my unborn baby! I made up my mind then. Time to resign from acting Coroner of Colquitt County. I refuse to do anything to put my unborn child at risk."

"It's that powerful, that drug that Susanna drank?"

"Lethal, Doc said. I don't know how she managed to even drive two miles from the rectory before she passed out at the wheel."

Royal sank back in his chair.

"Ah, Lorena! How are we supposed to find out what really happened now? You are part of the team, me, the sheriff, Doc

Huey, and that new guy, Keith. Four men who don't have a clue why or how my sister-in-law got the moonshine, or from whom. And why, for the love of God, would anyone want to kill off a nun?"

He stared at her, his eyes pleading. "Don't quit on us now, Lorena. You are, and have always been, the real brains of our pitiful little group."

She frowned as she thought about Susanna's death. "It is a big mystery, but I am sure you and the other men can figure it out, Royal."

"Not without you, Lorena, my dear."

"Now you sound like Doc Huey."

Royal leaned forward.

"How about this, Lorena? You stay on as Advisor to me, skip any 'wet work' in the autopsy room, and just plain help us figure out whatever puzzling death happens to come our way. For the duration, until your baby is born. Can you agree to that, at least?"

"Okay, Boss. But I will hold you to your promise of no autopsy work for me now."

Royal gave a great sigh of relief as he leaned back in his chair. He used one foot to swivel the chair back and forth for long moments before he finally, reluctantly, reached out and tapped the closed folder on the desk.

"Lorena? I assume that you reviewed this statement about Susanna's accident?"

She nodded. "Doc showed it to me, the autopsy part, as soon as he finished. Later that day, Lance filled me in on what he and Keith found at the scene."

Royal tapped the closed folder again.

"Yet, what they found in the wrecked car, doesn't seem to be a complete list of contents."

"What do you mean?" she asked, puzzled.

Royal fiddled a bit longer, tapping the folder and squeaking his swivel chair. He refused to meet Lorena's direct stare. Lorena leaned forward and touched his nervous fingers.

"Royal! Do you know something about this? What has you so nervous? It's not like you to be so twitchy."

"Ah, Lorena. People told me you never miss much when it comes to human behavior, especially when someone tries to cover up something about the newly dead." He sighed. "Guess they are right."

He leaned forward and lowered his voice to a whisper.

"Did they find any rosaries in Sister's purse, or in the car?"

Lorena's mouth dropped open. *Why on earth is Royal asking me about something like this? Wouldn't it be perfectly normal for a nun to keep rosaries in her purse? Never can tell when she might want to whip one out to pray for a needy soul along the way.*

She closed her mouth with a snap and cleared her throat.

"Why do you ask, Royal?"

He stared at the folder on the desk.

"It's just that my wife is missing her favorite rosary, the one that belonged to Amilee. She was in the habit of praying in our daughter's room every day. For comfort, you understand?"

His eyes pleaded for understanding as he finally met Lorena's sympathetic gaze.

"Royal, I don't believe the men found a rosary in the car. Lance mentioned what they did find in her purse: a small wallet with fifteen dollars inside, a few coins, a gas credit card, a half eaten candy bar, a few paper clips, and a rubber band. No rosary. Why would Susanna have Amilee's rosary, anyhow, if Mayree had possession of it in the first place?"

His glance burned fiercely.

"Because that meddling nun took it away from my wife. She had the *nerve* to tell Mayree that it was time for her to 'get over' all that weeping and wailing over our dead daughter!"

Lorena gasped. "How very thoughtless, even *cruel* of Susanna to torment her sister like that. True sorrow cannot be scolded away. It takes a long time for a parent who lost a child to stop grieving. Believe me, I have seen this many, many times. Some parents never 'get over' it. They go to their graves crippled by their loss."

Royal nodded. "*She* took *all* the rosaries in the house, even a collection that belonged to Mayree's mother. My wife is sick about it. And I am enraged! Frankly, Lorena, I don't care if we ever catch whoever killed Susanna. I believe this world is a better place without her."

Lorena stared at him, shocked. Yet, deep in her motherly heart, she sympathized with his strong emotion. Betrayal is a tough burden to swallow. And she knew both Mayree and Royal felt betrayed by Sister Susanna.

"Royal, I am so sorry about the rosaries, and about the pain your wife suffered because of her sister's harsh words. But I would be careful what you say about your 'holy' sister-in-law right now. She is newly deceased, and people might begin to think you or your wife had something to do with her tragic death if you go around sprouting off like this."

He seemed to shrink into his chair. His hands came up in a defensive posture.

"I didn't mean to sound so vengeful, it's just that anything that causes my wife more pain these days ... Well, I can't help being defensive about her."

"Yes, I realize that, Royal. And you know I will not spread any rumors about you or Mayree." She made the twisting of a key motion across her mouth. "My lips are sealed. I'll ask Lance this evening if they found any rosaries in the wreckage. He may have just forgotten to list them, him not being a member of our faith, you understand?"

Royal nodded his thanks. Moments later, Lorena folded herself into her personal vehicle, an oversized Ford S.U.V. The sweet scent of flowers lingered in the humid air of the car. It served to remind her that the car's main purpose was to deliver flowers to the church before a funeral. She sat behind the wheel and tapped her fingers against it for long moments as she contemplated Royal's words. Not so much his words, but the rage behind them.

"Rosaries? Stolen rosaries?"

People had been murdered for less reason than the cruel abuse of power over a dead child's rosary.

She started the car and drove home, her mind whirling as she contemplated the implications of Royal's angry words.

Chapter 30

Stuart

Stuart made tents of his fingers as he leaned across the pages of the parish ledger. For some reason, last Sunday's collection total had jumped several hundred dollars. He had leafed back to previous weekend totals from two months ago and the new larger amount almost matched them. But for several weeks before Sister's Susanna began her audit, the dollar amounts had dwindled by half. Now the collection baskets overflowed once more.

Somebody had been dipping into the till. Susanna's arrival must have scared him or her off. Now the financial situation is back to normal. He shook his head.

"Now how am I supposed to find out who's been helping themself to the collection basket?" he muttered aloud.

Monsignor McGaffee overheard Stuart's remarks as the pastor entered the room.

"So, the thief's been scared off, you think Mr. Bouton?" He heaved a long sigh of relief.

"For now, Father. But who can say it won't happen again, once I go back to my regular job and the books remain unattended?"

"Are you campaigning for job security, Stu?"

The pastor's voice sounded haughty. It made Stuart flush.

"No Sir! My salary at Lorena's establishment is more than generous. I really don't need a second job."

"But you didn't discover whose sticky fingers have been dipping into the church funds?"

Monsignor sounded almost hopeful. Stuart guessed the priest did not want a public scandal about thievery in his parish. *Bet the pastor would rather ignore the whole thing and hope it just goes away?* Stu leaned back in the soft leather chair. His shoulders hurt from bending over the account books. He sighed and swiped at his drippy nose.

"Father, I don't know what Sister Susanna found out about all this." He waved one hand over the open ledger. "But I did not discover the culprit from these facts and figures."

He heaved another reluctant sigh and reached for his tissue

"I do have some thoughts for you to dwell upon. One, the thief is connected to the rectory area. This is the only place where the collections are kept before the money-counters arrive Sunday evenings. Two, there are enough counters to keep track of each other. Somebody in your faithful group would have noticed even the most clever slight-of-hand artist shoving bills into a pocket or purse. Third, from the time the baskets are passed at Sunday services, until the money-counters arrive that evening, the money bags sit here, available for anyone who might pass by."

Stuart paused to swipe at his nose, running of course, as he laid out the unpopular facts to the looming Monsignor.

"But I keep this office locked!" the pastor protested.

"All the time. Every time?"

Monsignor's face clouded. His eyes shifted back and forth as he reviewed his ingrained habits.

"Well, sometimes, I unlock it so Kat can come in a straighten up in here. Dust, you know, and sometimes I track in mud and leaves from my walks in the cemetery."

His eyes widened.

"Surely you are not thinking about my housekeeper? Outrageous! She's been with me for twenty years now."

Stuart spread his hands and shrugged.

"There is also Seedy. He has an office down the hall. Wouldn't take but a minute for him to slip in and grab up a few bills while Mrs. T was distracted by a phone call or something."

"Deacon Ned? Impossible! He is a man of the cloth now."

Monsignor's face reflected scarlet outrage. Stuart dabbed at his nose again.

"I am only tossing out possibilities for you to think over, Monsignor. You know your people, I don't. Maybe if you talk to both of them? Maybe one at a time and check their stories for inadequacies? It's your parish and your employees, Father. I can only remind you that Seedy was going on and on about his Children's Saving Network the other day at lunch. He mentioned how great the need was, and how little funds he had to work with."

Stuart spread his hands and shrugged. He stood up to leave.

"My work is done here now. You can mail my salary, if you think I deserve one, to Magee's Mortuary. If you send a check to my home, my wife will snatch it up and spend it before the ink dries!"

Monsignor stopped Stuart by grabbing his arm.

"I sincerely trust that you will not report this to the authorities? I realize you work for the Coroner, Lorena McGee, and she is married now to Sheriff Lundrum. But this is a Church matter and I don't plan to file charges, at least not yet."

The pastor frowned and tapped his lips with one long finger.

"What happens at church, stays at church, is that what you are saying, Monsignor?"

The tall pastor nodded and bowed stiffly.

Stuart smiled at his weak joke and turned to leave. Monsignor did not offer his hand, or walk him to the door. Stuart's nose ran continuously the entire way back to McGee's Mortuary.

Chapter 31

The Rosary Mysteries

Lance and Lorena, in the privacy of their new bedroom, quietly discussed the mystery of Sister Susanna's untimely death.

"Truly, Lorena, Darlin', I am stumped about this nun's death. I mean, who would think a woman of God would drink high test moonshine?"

"And then wrap her car around a tree," Lorena said, shaking her head in disbelief.

"Have you talked to Royal? After all, his sister-in-law ..."

"Yes, I went over there today to resign from my Coroner's position, but he begged me to stay on as an advisor. He is as puzzled as we all are about his mess."

"Did you learn anything from him about Sister Susanna's last day?"

"He mentioned something strange about his wife's sister. Seems that the so called holy woman made life miserable for Mayree."

Lance sat up straighter. He had been lounging against the bed post as they sat side by side on their bed. His shrewd eyes narrowed as he leaned toward Lorena.

"Tell me what he said."

"Royal said Susanna yelled at Mayree after finding her praying the rosary in the little girl's bedroom."

Lance gasped, shocked.

"Not only that, that cruel woman yanked the rosary out of her sister's hands and wouldn't give it back. Told Mayree to stop weeping and wailing over her daughter's death. Royal was as shocked as you are, Lance. He also said Susanna took a box full of their mother's rosaries and hid them too. Mayree must be heartbroken."

Lorena's violet eyes grew as dark as the sky during a bad summer storm.

"Shame on that woman. A holy nun of God, acting with such malice toward her own sister. No wonder someone killed her."

"Do you really think Sister Susanna was murdered, Lorena? After all, she drank the moonshine herself, don't you think?"

Lorena sank back into the pillows behind her. She folded her arms over the baby bump and shuddered.

"Doc Huey said she must have been in a coma when she hit that tree. But what I can't get my head around is why she would drink such a potent brew in the first place? Surely the strong smell of it would warn her the shine must have been altered in some way. And the taste! I heard old Jimmy John, the moonshiner, tell me good shine has little or no real taste, or odor for that matter. Jimmy John said, 'Good shine just slips down your throat until it hits your belly. Then it feels like you drank down a fiery lump of coal!'"

Lance scowled. "Yep, Jimmy John was proud of his brew all right. Got him sent up to Federal prison, too." His face darkened as he remembered the circumstances of Jimmy John's arrest. "Good thing the Feds took him when they did, before I wrung his scrawny neck!"

Lorena patted his fists. "My hero," she said softly.

"But that still leaves the mystery of why or where she got the shine in the first place. Did I tell you we found a crushed flask in the wreckage of the car?"

"A flask? Strange thing for a nun to carry in her purse." Lorena tapped her lips in deep thought. "Maybe she stole it from May-ree?"

Lance frowned. "Never thought of that part, where the flask came from. But when we went over the evidence from the wrecked car with the D.A., Royal got pretty upset. In fact, he rushed to the bathroom and lost his breakfast. Both Keith and I heard him retching, even with that thick oak door closed behind him."

"Maybe you need another conversation with Royal?"

"Ah, Lorena. You and that fine brain of your's. I knew, once we got together and compared notes, you would think of something important."

Lance swept her into his arms for a long hug. The kiss that followed served to wipe away all thoughts of murder or mayhem from their minds.

Chapter 32

Stuart

Next morning Lorena found Stuart hard at work in their shared office at McGee's Mortuary. He glanced up as she entered the room. His nose was running.

"Morning Stu. Something wrong? I see you need a tissue already and it's not even nine o'clock. Money problems?"

Stuart flushed and swiped at his nose. "Sorry, Lorena. No, nothing wrong here." He tapped the ledger in front of him. "Your recent out-flow of money barely touches the interest from your investments, as usual." He reached for another tissue.

"What is it then? Blanche ready to bankrupt you again," she said with a gentle smile.

He shook his head. "No more than usual, Lorena. But I am worried about our family."

"Oh?" She sat down, ready to listen to whatever family drama had Stuart so upset.

"It's Harlan. You know he sold the mill? Well now, whenever we call to check up on him, he tells us, 'I'm just sitting here waiting to die.' Blanche and I think he is suicidal."

"Poor Harlan. He took Bunny's death pretty hard. Remember how he collapsed at his wife's Wake? You and Uncle Morley had to carry him out. Good thing Raysa went with him that night or he might be dead already, by his own hand." She shook her head.

Stuart's nose ran faster. "We believe he has lost his will to live."

"What can we do to help him?" Lorena asked. "Has Doc Huey been over to see him lately?"

"Huey tried, but Harlan didn't even have the common courtesy to answer the door."

Lorena sighed and spread her hands. "Then there is little anyone can do to help him short of committing him to a mental hospital."

"Blanche already looked into that. There is a nice facility just outside Autryville. Harlan flatly refused to even consider it. He seems determined to waste his life away, waiting for his dead wife to come back and rescue him from the trials and tribulations of this world."

"Sounds like something Harlan would say." Lorena sighed again. "Lordy I hate to think about hosting another family funeral! Haven't we suffered enough death in the family already?"

She burst into tears.

Stuart, alarmed by his employer's outburst, went to her side and awkwardly patted her shoulder. "Now, now Lorena. I'm sorry I upset you. It's just not like you to get so upset. Are you all right? Should I call Doc or Raysa for you?"

She sniffed and reached for one of his tissues, kept always handy on his desk.

"Sorry, Stu. Hope I didn't scare you, acting like a pregnant woman just now." Her smile wobbled. She swiped at her eyes. "Don't know why I keep getting so emotional these days." She patted her belly. "But I think Junior here has something to do with it."

"Maybe the baby is a girl. I heard that little girls cry a lot. Not that I would know. My daughter was raised by Blanche. I was too busy working as a school teacher to pay her much mind. Now I wish I had paid her more attention. Maybe she might come around once in a while." He reached for another tissue.

Lorena patted his hand. "Ah, Stu. Parents always carry so much guilt over our past mistakes, don't we?"

He sighed and nodded. He watched Lorena for long moments before she finally straightened up in her chair.

"I'll talk to Raysa and Doc about Harlan. Maybe between all of us, we might be able to do something good for Harlan."

"Thanks Lorena. I knew we could count on you."

Chapter 33

Harlan

Harlan ignored the loud knocking as long as he could. Finally, sighing deeply, he arose from his recliner and staggered to the front door. Leaning against the frame for balance, he jerked open the heavy door. He favored the little group of kin folk on his porch with a fierce scowl.

"What? Why can't you people just leave me alone?"

Doc Huey pushed past him, followed by Raysa and Lorena. The little group entered the large sitting room and stopped abruptly, astonished at the untidy messes piled here and there in the cavernous room. Huey took a stab at humor.

"So what happened here, Harlan? Someone break in on you, hunting for treasure?"

Harlan hovered in the doorway, still clinging to the frame for balance. His haggard face drew back into wrinkles of outrage.

"No! Nobody here but me. And nobody invited you people to bust in here and criticize my housekeeping! Get out! Now!"

Raysa reached toward his arm in a comforting gesture. He drew back so quickly, he staggered, almost falling to the oak parquet floor of the foyer.

"Leave me alone. Just leave me alone to die!"

Lorena spoke quietly. "Harlan. We are here to help you, not hurt you. We are family, not enemies. No one is judging you."

Harlan slid to the floor, sobbing. "I can't go on, Lorena. Not without Bunny. It's just too hard." He covered his face with trembling fingers. "Just too hard without my sweetheart."

Doc and Raysa helped Lorena lift Harlan to his feet. They walked the man, his legs buckling under him, to a nearby chair. Raysa hurried to the kitchen for a cold cloth. As she swiped Harlan's face, she glanced at Doc for further advice.

"Usually I would recommend a shot of something strong, Princess, but I reckon Harlan has imbibed too much already," Huey said.

Raysa nodded. She stared around at the messes, piles of crumpled newspaper, and discarded, obviously dirty, clothing, shirts, pants, even underwear. Empty bottles of bourbon, whiskey, and even an occasional bottle of gin, Bunny's favored drink, were shattered against the fireplace. Glass shards littered the Oriental rug.

Amazing how much of a mess a man can make in just a couple of months when left to his own devices. Or vices!

Lorena spoke up. "So, what now, Doc? The man is obviously bent on self-destruction. Can't we all, acting as family members, sign him into a mental facility? He truly needs help. Anybody can see that."

"I don't know, my dear," Doc Huey said slowly. "Do we have the right to interfere like that?"

Raysa unwrapped a slice of cinnamon gum and popped it into her mouth, a sure sign she felt nervous and upset. She said, "I think we not only have the right, we have the *obligation* to help him."

A commotion behind them caught their attention. As a group, they whirled around. Harlan had slipped from his chair onto the floor. He began to writhe, his whole body convulsing. Foam slid from his mouth as his eyes rolled up until they showed only the white. All three people fell to their knees. They reached quickly to turn the stricken man onto one side. Lorena jumped up to grab pillows off a couch to slide behind his back in order to prop him into that position. The seizure ended as quickly as it began.

By the time Harlan's eyes began to flutter open, Doc had called an ambulance. The stricken man offered no resistance as the EMT's lifted him onto a stretcher and carried him away.

Doc Huey signed the admittance papers.

"Mr. Parnell needs 24/7 monitoring," he instructed the ambulance crew. "Take him to the hospital in Autryville. He needs more help than we can give him here."

Huey stood in the doorway of Harlan's mansion. On either side of the aging physician, Raysa and Lorena completed the group hug. All three people fought back tears as the ambulance pulled away, sirens blaring.

A few hours later, Lorena's cell phone rang. The news from Autreyville hospital made her sink into the nearest chair.

"Sorry, Ma'am. Mr. Parnell flat-lined in the ambulance. Our blood tests showed he died of alcohol poisoning. I understand he has no next of kin, other than in-laws. What do you want us to do with the remains?"

Lorena swiped tears from her cheeks with the sleeve of her blouse. It took her a moment to compose herself enough to reply.

"Alcohol poisoning? Did the test show any signs of isopropanol?"

"No, Ma'am. Just regular liquor as far as I know, a deadly amount of alcohol in his system. Was he suicidal?"

"That poor man. After his wife died, he just lost his will to live."

"So … his remains?"

"I am the Coroner here, and the only mortician available. I will send someone down to pick up Mr. Parnell this evening."

"Thanks Ma'am. I have heard about you and the kind way you always take care of the deceased. Are you one of his in-laws?"

"Well, sort of. Don't worry, the family lawyer will be involved in all this. Morley Wilton has already been told of Harlan's illness."

Lorena folded her phone. She held it between her palms for long moments, head bent, saying a sad prayer for the repose of Harlan's soul. Then she stood up, squared her shoulders, and called Keith. She felt sure he would drive to Autreyville for her and pick up Harlan's body.

"Another family funeral," she said, and burst into tears again.

Chapter 34

Hannah

The office door stood open, so Hannah wheeled the vacuum cleaner into the room. She bent down to plug it into the nearest duplex, when the bathroom door creaked open. Startled, Hannah jumped back, cord in hand, and yanked the plug out of the wall outlet.

"Ssssorry, Mr. Taylor," she stammered and turned to flee.

"Hannah! Wait!" Taylor yelled.

His apologetic expression revealed a deep desire to kick himself as he stared at her flushed face. He held out one hand toward her and lowered his voice. His piercing blue stare softened.

"Please, Hannah. I just want a word or two with you."

He gestured toward the "visitor's chair" in front of his desk. Hannah dragged her reluctant feet forward. She felt like a death row inmate being introduced to the electric chair. Heaving a long, frightened sigh, Hannah collapsed into the richly padded seat. She stared at her hands, deeply clenched in her lap.

Royal sat down opposite her, the big desk between them. Hannah noticed the desk top needed dusting. She blushed at her neglect. *Will he fire me now?* she wondered, not for the first time.

"I'm sssssorry, Mr. Taylor," she began, trying to postpone the words she dreaded to hear.

Royal sighed and drummed his thin fingers on the desk. She stared, ashamed at the proof of her neglect: his fingers raising puffs of dust. She began to apologize again, but he lifted both narrow hands, fingers spread.

"Please, Hannah. No more apologies. I just need some information."

He leaned toward her. Those sharp blue eyes demanded the truth. But Hannah did appreciate the way he tried to keep his voice calm and non threatening.

"Hannah, do you have any idea who might have given Sister Susanna the moonshine that killed her?"

She gasped and leaned back. Even the soft comfort of the chair, cradling her aching bones, did not ease her flare of fear. Reluctantly, Hannah nodded. She opened her mouth to speak, but only impotent sputters echoed in the quiet room.

Royal slid the yellow legal pad toward her and provided a pen.

She sat up straighter and began to write. Soon she could slide the pad toward her employer, and give a smug satisfied smile. *This ought to fix those Kemper brothers,* she thought. *Trying to hurt that poor Petey.*

She watched as Royal quickly scanned the words. His eyebrows lifted as he looked up to stare directly into Hannah's eyes.

"You sure about this, Hannah? Clyde and Joey Kemper gave our paperboy moonshine in a Mountain Dew bottle?"

Hannah nodded. "Hooligans!" she said.

It felt wonderful, being able to say the word without stuttering.

Royal smiled and looked pleased at her success with the spoken word, too. Then he frowned. Wrinkles warped his forehead.

"So what happened to that bottle of shine, Hannah?"

"I gggggot rid of it," she said and stared at her hands again.

She waited for the next question, but it never came that day. Later, she would regret not going into detail about how she got rid of the moonshine.

I should have told him more, she thought later. *After all my employer is the District Attorney of Colquitt County.*

But Royal, apparently satisfied with a clue, *finally*, on who might have made and/or distributed the high test shine, stood up and smiled.

"I'll use the kitchen phone to call the Sheriff," he said, "so you can run the vacuum here." He waved vaguely around the room. "Carry on."

"Tell Mayree I will be back later," he said and walked away. "Need to fetch the Sheriff and see your *hooligans* about some doctored shine."

Hannah leaped to her feet, raced to her cleaning supplies, and brought out a can of furniture polish and a cleaning rag. She worked vigorously that day, spit-shining all surfaces in the Boss's office. She smiled gratefully as she worked herself into a sweat over her chores.

Thank God he didn't fire me this time.

Chapter 35

Royal and Lance

"Now Royal, before we go question the Kemper brothers, we have something else to discuss. I have a strong hunch that you know more than you are letting on."

The District Attorney bristled. "What do you mean, Lance?"

They faced each other across the Sheriff's scarred desk. Lance leaned back and put his big booted feet on the corner of the desk. He plucked at one long denim clad pant leg and crossed his feet. Royal noticed the ankle holster peeking just above the long leather boots the sheriff wore.

"What was all that commotion after Keith and I mentioned the flask we found in wreckage of the nun's car?"

Royal's face drained of color. He bit his lips and said nothing.

"Now, Royal. Even your expression tells me a lot. Looking pretty guilty right now, Mr. D.A."

Royal spread his hands and sighed. "I think that flask was mine, a family heirloom. I never used it, just kept it in my desk at home. I never even noticed it was missing, until I read your accident report."

"But why did it affect you so much that you tossed your cookies when you read about it?"

The District Attorney flushed and stared at the clenched fists in his lap. He relaxed his fingers with a visible effort of will.

"I thought maybe my wife …"

Lance's boots hit the floor as he leaned across the desk.

"You thought maybe your wife was using your flask?"

Royal shrugged. His face drained of color. "I didn't know what was going on. Nobody even told me how Mayree and her sister had a big fight Sunday night until much later. I didn't even realize that Susanna took my wife's rosaries away from her! Maybe she found my flask and stole that, too! I just don't know!"

He buried his face in his hands and struggled not to weep.

"My wife has been through so much … losing our daughter … putting up with that shrew of a sister … I just don't know what happened."

Lance leaned forward and drew a deep breath before he asked the million dollar question.

"Do you think Mayree might have poisoned her sister?"

Royal peeked through his spread fingers. Horror darkened his blue eyes to a deep navy shade. "I don't know. I just don't know. And God help me, I am afraid to ask her about it!"

The Sheriff sank back in his chair. He drew a deep breath as he stared across his scarred desk at Royal Taylor. He cleared his throat, a startling sound in the too quiet room. The District Attorney jumped and dropped his shaking fingers into his lap.

"Uh, Taylor, maybe you might better not come with me to question the Kemper boys. Not a good idea now, with you so worked up and all. Might scare those hoodlums into permanent muteness, if you catch my drift?"

Taylor nodded. "You're right, Lance. I just might muddy the waters, so to speak, if I grabbed up one of those boys and shook the living hell out of 'em."

"I'll get Keith to go with me. Might teach the kid something about how we enforce the law in these parts."

"Down home justice is a whole 'nother animal than military law, right Sheriff?"

"Damn straight!"

Chapter 36

Stuart

The office door banged open and John-Duncan lumbered in at trot, his face twisted with anguish. *Well, at least nobody can claim John ever tried to sneak up on a body,* Stuart thought, then felt ashamed of his reaction to the boy's sudden entrance. He sat up straighter and put his accounting papers aside.

"What is it, John-Duncan?"

"Mama's crying."

"What? Why?"

Stu reached for a tissue to blot his nose. He marveled at the beautiful mystery of a pregnant woman, so easily prone to tears.

The boy/man flapped his hands in agitation.

"Mama's crying. Grandma Belle says, 'Come!'"

Immediately, his nose streaming, Stuart stood and followed John-Duncan out the door toward the stairway. The boy did not even pause to use the chair lift, a favored activity for a fun-loving kid, but raced up the steps, his heavy tread rattling the wood.

Stuart followed, mystified. *What happened?* His heart sank at the sudden thought, *Is Lorena losing her baby?* He found Lorena and Belle, the housekeeper, huddled together on the couch in the living room. Both women were rocking and weeping. He stood before them, almost afraid to speak, dreading what they might tell him.

Belle looked up first.

"Mr. Bouton, thank God you are here!" she blurted, her words running together.

Her eyes, reddened with tears, glanced beyond him to the boy, pacing in and out of the room, hands flapping.

"Johnny, sit down now. Mama is all right. Mr. Bouton will help us."

Stuart watched as Lorena struggled to regain her composure. When she could speak, her voice sounded raw and hoarse.

"It's Harlan. He died in the ambulance on the way to Autreyville Hospital. I tried to call Keith and Lance, but both men are off investigating some kids accused of making high test shine."

She swallowed hard and swiped at her cheeks with the back of her hand, a heartbroken child mourning the loss of a beloved family member.

Stuart cleared his throat. "I am sorry about Harlan, Lorena. I assumed he wouldn't live long after losing Bunny. I heard he had turned into a hermit. Even refused to answer the door when Blanche went over with some food for him."

He swiped at his nose, staring as Lorena continued to weep, her beautiful violet eyes dark with sorrow.

"I didn't realize you felt so close to our brother-in-law, Lorena. He never seemed very kind to you, or to any of us, truth be told."

She shook her head and reached for a nearby tissue.

"It's not that so much, losing another family member, it's just ..."

Belle spoke up. "Lorena needs someone to drive the hearse to Autreyville and pick up Harlan's body. She wanted Keith to do it, but ..."

"But nobody is available to go? Is that why you two are so broken up?"

Stuart shuffled his feet and cleared his throat.

"I can do it. Drive to the hospital and pick up Harlan, if that's what you need."

Both women leaped to their feet and gave him a group hug.

"Thanks so much, Stu!" Lorena said. "I didn't know what to do. This silly weeping and wailing is just getting out of hand. I can barely function anymore."

He patted both women on their backs, trying not to be awkward about it. He did not feel comfortable with all this hugging and high emotion surrounding him.

"Where are the keys to your hearse, Lorena? And what do I need to take with me? Paperwork, a release form? I never drove a hearse before."

Just the thought of all those miles to Autreville and back, while Harlan's dead body rattled around behind him, made Stu shiver with anticipated dread. He had heard stories of "dead" people suddenly sitting up. What if he felt a clammy hand on his shoulder as he drove through the darkness? His heart thumped in his chest at the frightening thought. He reached for a tissue as his nose sprouted a new gush of fluid. He stared at his highly polished shoes. A dribble of nose fluid dotted the surface of his right shoe. He bent down to swipe it away with his soggy tissue. When he straightened up, red of face and embarrassed, he felt Lorena's hand on his arm.

"Stu, you don't have to do this if you don't want to. I am used to transporting the newly dead. It doesn't bother me anymore. I could go myself but I am afraid these 'baby blues' might start up again and distract me from a safe journey."

They stared at each other for long moments. Stuart did want to beg off, but he loved Lorena like a sister and did not want any harm to come to her or her baby.

"How about this," Lorena said. "You drive and I'll ride shot-gun?"

Her smile wobbled.

"I can do the paperwork and sign the release forms too, once we get there. How about it, Stu?" She punched his arm playfully."Together we can fight those woolly boogies of yours."

"Sure Lorena. We can go together."

He stared at his shoes. No more dribbles marred their high polish.

"And thanks," he whispered.

Chapter 37

The Journey

Stuart climbed behind the wheel of the long black vehicle used always to transport the deceased. The steering wheel felt spongy beneath his sweating fingers. Quickly drying them on his knees, he turned toward Lorena.

"Ready to go, Sis?"

She smiled. "Thanks Stu. Usually Blanche and Raysa are the only ones who call me Sis. Sounds nice coming from you all of a sudden. Usually you are pretty formal around the office."

He faked a thin grin. "Well this is a special occasion. Not every night I get to go traveling with such a good looking female. Thought I better remind myself of our family ties."

It was whistle in the dark talk, he realized, but it did feel comforting to him non-the-less.

Lorena laughed away his compliment and patted her swollen abdomen.

"Better enjoy it while you can. This old mama won't be good looking much longer if this hungry babe keeps growing so fast."

He started up the hearse and drove down the long driveway. Turning right, they headed toward Autreyville hospital. The ride seemed long and too silent for both of them. After ten minutes, Stuart cleared his throat. Lorena turned to him, waiting. Sometimes it took a while before Stu spoke his mind.

"Lorena? What did the doctors say about Harlan's cause of death? I thought you mentioned alcohol poisoning."

"'Acute alcohol poisoning,' the resident told me."

A heavy silence hung over both of them. Lorena stared out the side window. Stu watched the empty road ahead.

"You don't think …?"

Both of them blurted out their most dreaded fear.

Stuart reached for tissues, kept in the console between the front seats. Lorena stared at him in the semi-darkness of the dashboard lights. She spoke first, her voice faint as she hesitated to mention what had haunted her since she first heard about Harlan's death.

"Alcohol poisoning? Surely Stu, you don't think Harlan drank the same high test moonshine that killed Sister Susanna?"

He shrugged. The hearse swerved a bit, then straightened up.

"I don't know what to think, Lorena! Two deaths in the same week? Both from acute alcohol poisoning?"

He clamped his hands around the steering wheel and stared straight ahead.

Lorena's soft question did not stop his nose from running fluently.

"Could we have a serial killer on the loose in Colquitt County?"

"Surely not, Lorena. Surely not!"

He pried one hand loose from the steering wheel to grab up a fistful of tissues.

They remained silent for most of the remaining trip. As Stuart pulled into the loading dock at the hospital, she turned to him.

"Looks as if Huey will need to do another autopsy."

He nodded as he shut down the motor, then collapsed against the back of the seat.

"Do you mind if I stay in the car until you bring out the body, Lorena?"

She patted his clammy hand. "Sure, Stu. Want me to bring you a Coke to fortify you for the return journey?"

"I need something stronger than that to buck me up, Sis. But Coke will be fine, thanks."

Chapter 38

The Kemper Brothers

Keith clung to the passenger door of the Sheriff's old pickup. His white-knuckled grip on the door handle made it jiggle. It felt loose. He worried it might break off in his hands, leaving him sprawled across the bench seat. Beside him, bouncing along, his long lean joints absorbing the roughness of the deeply rutted mud road, Lance chuckled. The deep rumble in his throat failed to reassure his nervous deputy.

"You might better let loose of that handle before you disable it, Son," Lance said, and chuckled again.

Keith gritted his teeth. "Better a broken handle than a fractured skull, Sheriff," he said. "Can't you at least slow down on this wreck of a road?"

"Want to sneak up on those Kemper folks, Son. If they see us coming from afar off, they will melt into the woods. Mark my words, we might never find them if they do. They are famous for their hidy-holes."

Keith turned to stare. "Really? How come?"

"Moonshiners. Third generation of shine brewers. Nobody dares to 'explore' their woods without those sniffer dogs the Feds have. Booby traps everywhere."

Keith, who had faced mortal combat in Iraq and managed to come home in one piece, felt unfamiliar fear raise the hair on the back of his neck. He cranked down the window and clung to its frame as they bounced along. Eyes ahead, he spotted a rustic cabin looming in the distance. Lance upped the speed. They pulled into a small clearing. The Sheriff hit the breaks and shut off the motor as they coasted the final few feet. He leaped out of the truck before it stopped, yanking his long-barreled pistol out of his holster as he trotted toward the porch. Keith had to hustle to keep up. Their boots thundered up the rickety steps. Lance yanked the screen door aside and entered the dim room.

An older couple glanced up from the kitchen table. Neither registered surprise at the sudden appearance of men with guns drawn, weapons pointed in their direction. Two teenaged boys leaped to their feet, ready to run.

"Clyde! Joey! Sit down. Can't you see the Sheriff is here for a friendly visit?"

"Aw Ma!" the boys protested as they sank back onto their wooden chairs.

Lance managed to tip his Stetson toward the woman, while still eyeing the man of the house with a narrowed, suspicious glare.

"Mrs. Kemper," he drawled politely. "Huck," he said and nodded stiffly toward Mr. Kemper.

Huck Kemper. Long arms propped on bony elbows, skinny legs clad in thin ancient jeans, big feet barely covered in ragged boots, he tipped back in his chair. He tossed thin, greasy hair off his face with a quick jerk of his narrow head. He grinned insolently.

"Been a while, Sheriff, since you paid us a visit."

He sucked on a chicken bone before tossing it toward his plate. His small dark eyes narrowed. He glanced at his wife, a large placid woman calmly chewing on a chicken wing. Nothing stopped Mrs. Kemper from enjoying her dinner. House on fire? Nothing worth saving here, she knew from sad experience. Lawmen busting into their home with guns drawn? Nothing unusual. Food was too hard to come by these days to let it get cold while men sorted out their business. She did jump when her husband's voice spoke in that dangerously low tone that meant a painful beating if she said something that riled him.

"Martha? I don't remember you telling me you invited our old friend, Lance here, to visit today."

She shrugged in a thin show of indifference and stared at her plate. Congealed chicken fat cooled as she dropped the chicken bone. Martha drew a deep calming breath.

"Didn't invite him, Huck. Guess he invited himself here."

She glanced at the Sheriff, fear flickering in her faded blue eyes.

Huck pushed back his chair. "Well, I guess I just better un-invite him, then."

"Sit down, Huck. We don't want any trouble with you. We just want to talk to your boys, there."

Lance waved his long pistol toward the teenagers. They stiffened, their eyes flickering back and forth, ready to bolt if they got the chance. Clyde, tall and skinny as his father, reached up to rake his thick red hair with thin, shaky fingers. Joey, the youngest, plump as his Ma, slouched over his paunch. But the freckles on his rounded cheeks blazed with guilt. When their Pa swung his narrowed gaze toward them, both boys stiffened in their seats. They raised their hands as if to deny whatever charges of mischief might be flung in their direction.

After a long glare at his sons, Huck turned back to the Sheriff.

"What have the kids been up to now? Must be pretty important for you dudes to come in here with weapons drawn."

He stared pointedly at the pistols in both Keith and Lance's hands.

Slowly Lance lowered his gun. Keith did the same. Neither man holstered his weapon but they no longer aimed them directly at the people at the table. Keith spoke up.

"All we want is to talk to Clyde and Joey. They might have important information to help us solve a murder."

"Murder!" Martha said, alarmed. "My boys ain't no murderers!"

"Never said they were, " Lance snapped.

"Just need some information, that's all, Mrs. Kemper," Keith said.

"What murder?" Huck said. "Didn't hear nothin' about no murder around these parts lately."

Lance shifted from one foot to the other. His feet burned. Maybe the priest's housekeeper was right: time for new boots. Or maybe he had laid on the gas pedal a little too hard driving in? In the brief silence, while Lance curled his aching toes, Keith spoke up again.

"The sister of our District Attorney died from drinking doctored up shine."

"Oh, you mean that nun from down Mississippi way? I heard something about that. Didn't she wrap her car around a tree?" Martha said.

Her faded eyes grew wide with wonder.

"And she was drinking shine? I thought those nun women were too good for drinking and carrying on. Never thought a woman of God would take up drinking common shine."

Her sons snickered. Their grins faded quickly as their father whirled to give them a deadly glare.

"There's nothing common about good grade moonshine," he thundered.

"As you well know, don't you Huck?" Lance said.

Huck's voice took on a nervous whine that seemed to astonish his wife and sons. All three of them stared at him, mouths agape.

"Now Lance. You know I'm done with all that stuff now. Turned over a new leaf after Jimmy John got busted by the Feds. No sir-ee-bob, no more cooking up shine for me."

He waved his hands, erasing an invisible blackboard. When his boys snickered again, he reached to unbuckle his belt. The glare he flung their way made them dwindle in their chairs.

Lance sighed. "We are not here to dig up Stills, old or new, Huck. We just need some information. Your boys could be heros, helping us solve this mystery. Come on, the D.A. remembers people who help him out. Never know when you might need to call in a favor, hmmm? How about it? Can we at least talk to your boys?"

The brothers stood and reluctantly came around the table to stand before the Sheriff and his deputy. Staring at their feet, the story the boys told them was long and complicated. It did little to solve how Sister Susanna came to drink high test shine from Royal Taylor's heirloom flask.

The Kemper brothers had found a green plastic bottle of Mountain Dew flung into the weeds along their dirt lane where it met highway 31.

"At first, we figured some collage kids were trying to outrun the cops and flung it out the window so they wouldn't get caught with something," Joey said. "You know how skittish those rich kids are about getting caught, right Sheriff?"

The younger brother dared to lift his head to meet the lawman's eyes.

Lance nodded curtly. "Go on."

The boys noticed the bottle top was tight, so they assumed it was just soda pop.

"Now who would just waste a perfectly good bottle of soda pop?" Clyde said.

When they opened it and took a swig, their eyes bugged out. The shine was too strong for kids not used to drinking alcohol. They spent the rest of the day puking behind the outhouse. Half of the bottle's liquor still remained, so they capped it up and tried to think of someone to play a trick on. Joey thought it might work better if they had a full bottle.

"Cause only a fool would drink from an opened bottle, right Sheriff? I mean, dirt and other stuff might be in there. Smart guys might think twice about drinking from somebody else's slobber, right?"

Lance sighed and nodded. "Go on, Joey. What did you do then?"

"Ma has some rubbing alcohol she uses when we get cut up in the brush. Stings like a fire ant's bite, but Ma says it keeps out the germs. Anyway, it was alcohol, right? So we filled the green bottle with the rubbing alcohol."

"And then?" Lance said, though he knew the answer already.

Good thing he had talked to Royal before they left for the Kemper shack. The D.A.'s conversation with Hannah had shed a lot of light on this twisted mystery.

Joey hung his head again before he answered. "Then we gave it to that dummy Petey, the paperboy who rides around on his fancy bicycle like he's king of the road."

"And you told him it would cure what ails him, right?" Lance said, jabbing the boy in his flabby belly.

Joey winced at the pain of Lance's calloused finger poking his gut. He tried to draw back.

"We didn't mean him no harm, Sheriff. It was just a joke, that's all."

Martha gasped. "Is that poor retarded boy all right?" she said. "I didn't hear nothin' about him getting sick." Her voice trailed away.

Lance stared from one brother to the other, both boys shivering in their shoes. He shook his head, afraid to let loose the cuss words he longed to shout at them. Wordlessly, he stared at Huck. The boys' father nodded. An unspoken agreement flashed between them. Huck unbuckled his belt.

As Keith and Lance closed the screen door behind them, both heard the yelps of Clyde and Joey as their Pa swung his belt. Moments later, a screen door out back slammed as two boys streaked across a back yard littered with old tires and crippled appliances. Long-legged Clyde leaped over the obstacles. Joey, heavier and slower, stumbled a crooked path through the litter. The angry shouts of their parents did not slow down their escape.

"Never mind, Huck," Martha said. "They'll be back come suppertime. You know boys, they never miss a meal."

Keith climbed into the truck. As he fastened his seatbelt, he turned to Lance.

"Some heros!" he said bitterly. "Why didn't we arrest them for giving alcohol to a minor? Those hoodlums need a stern punishment. Where is the justice?"

Lance paused as he slid the key into the ignition. His grin twisted his mouth into a frown.

"Don't worry, Keith. Those boys will get 'justice' from Huck when he catches up with them. Even moonshiners have their pride. No one wants their sons to be labeled cruel or heartless. Puts a shame on the family in their close knit group of outlaws and rednecks."

Keith sank back against the torn seat. He grabbed the door frame as Lance stomped on the gas. He shook his head. "Moonshiner's justice. A new one on me."

Lance reached across the seat and punched him on the upper arm.

"You're new at this yet, Bucko. Give it time, you'll adjust."

Keith wanted to rub the sore spot on his upper arm. Stung pretty good, that friendly punch from his boss. But as the truck rocketed across the rut-pocked road, he didn't dare let loose of the door frame.

Chapter 39

Stuart

Both Lorena and Stuart were yawning as they arrived back at McGee's Mortuary. As Stu slowly drove up the long driveway, Lorena waved him toward the large building behind the house.

"Just pull in the turn-around and back up to the garage door."

She reached across the seat, leaning toward him as she pressed the garage door opener attached to the sunshade. Stuart watched in the mirror as the tall white automatic door slowly rumbled up. It rattled a bit as it hit the top frame, then quieted, a familiar robot waiting further instructions.

"Do you want me to back in?" Stuart said.

"No, I'll fetch a gurney." she unbuckled her seat belt and slid out of the vehicle. Leaning back into the car, she asked, "Maybe you could help me make the transfer? Used to be, I could do all that muscle work without help, but now …" She gestured toward the baby bump visible beneath her long sweater.

"Sure. No problem," he said and shut off the engine.

His heart thumped in his chest, a reminder that he would be touching a *corpse*, the remains of his brother-in-law. But the voice of common sense quieted his fear. *Buck up, Stuart! You don't want to look like a pansy, like a kid afraid of a zombie in front of Lorena, do you?* Sweating with nerves, his nose dripping like mad, he managed to assuage his dread as the two of them slid the dead body, encased in a black plastic bag, from the back of the hearse and onto the gurney.

Lorena's smile sagged with fatigue. She swiped sweat from her forehead as Stuart dabbed at his streaming nose. They worked together, rolling the gurney through a door that led directly into the refrigerated "work room" of the mortuary. A ceiling light flickered on as the door opened. Stu jumped, alarmed at the sudden blaze of light.

Lorena smiled. "Duncan, my adoptive father, installed that automatic light switch thirty years ago. How proud he had been at his cleverness! 'No more bumping into walls in the dark, my pretty child,' he told me. I remember his sweet smile as he beamed down on me."

She heaved a long tired sigh. "I still miss him."

Stuart patted her back. She straightened and gave a little shudder as if to shake off old memories.

"Let's push this over under the center lights, OK? I'll call Huey in the morning."

"Do you want me to call Morley for you, Lorena?"

"Thanks Stu. I dread dealing with that stiff-necked lawyer. Sometimes Morley relishes his role as family solicitor a bit too much. He always loves to denigrate me to that orphan child, hanging onto Duncan's knee. Don't need that now, especially with another family funeral to plan."

Chapter 40

Funeral Plans

Lorena sighed as she listened to the pompous voice of Morley Wilton. His deep voice rumbled through the kitchen phone like the voice of God damning her soul to eternal hellfire. It held a hypnotic drone that almost lulled her to sleep. She yawned.

Short night, she thought. *I need a nap! Scant good it did for Stuart to call the family solicitor if Morley just turned around and called me with this harangue.*

After a long silence, his voice jerked her from a half doze.

"Hello? Are you there, Lorena?"

"Of course, *Mister* Wilton! Where else would I be, other than here hanging onto your every golden word?"

She bit her lip. *That sounded a bit more sarcastic than I planned. Sleep starved, that must be it. Poor excuse for being rude,* she thought and blushed.

Morley gasped, then, surprisingly, laughed.

"Sorry, Lorena. I do tend to pontificate now and then. Forgot you are family. And I do appreciate your spunk! Thanks for the wake-up call."

"What were you saying, anyway? I got a bit lost in all the legalize language. Almost dozed off. Remember, my 'delicate condition'?" Her turn to laugh.

His voice softened. "Nothing of any big importance for right now. I understand Doc Huey did the Post Mortem? Anything suspicious, like poison in his throat?"

"No, just a bit of cancer in his liver. Basically, Harlan drank himself to death."

"So, there is nothing to prevent his remains from burial in the traditional sense?"

"Nothing. Did Harlan indicate anything specific about his funeral plans?"

Morley cleared his throat. She heard the rattle of paper as he shuffled through Harlan's last Will and Testament. The lawyer had mentioned earlier that Harlan had drawn up new instructions a month before, shortly after his beloved wife, Bunny, had died.

"He was very emphatic about his funeral, especially the Wake. Closed coffin, only one short Viewing before being interred beside his beloved wife."

"Closed coffin?" she said. "So a non-traditional Wake then?"

Morley cleared his throat. "Harlan said, 'I don't want people gawking at me. Some of them, maybe the people I had to lay off when I closed the Mill, might even want to spit on me. Tell Lorena to keep my coffin closed!'"

"All right, Morley. When should I plan all this? Tomorrow? Saturday? Next Monday?"

"No need to delay, my dear. How many people will even come to his Wake anyway? He left no family other than the Wilton sisters." He cleared his throat. "I'll fly down tomorrow."

"Need a ride from the airport?"

"No, I can rent a car."

"I'll plan the funeral for Saturday, then. OK?"

"See you then. I can bunk with Stuart and Blanche."

Lorena hung up. She lingered so long at the kitchen phone, leaning against the cupboard in a near-daze, that Belle came to her side.

"Miss Lorena, you need to sit down now. Maybe even take a nap. You look darned near exhausted."

Lorena yawned again. She smiled at her friend and house-keeper.

"I think I just might do that, take a nap, that is. Feel a mite bit tuckered. I can take care of Harlan's body later, after lunch. Maybe even tomorrow."

She followed obediently as Belle urged her down the hallway to their new bedroom. Belle threw back the comforter. Kicking off her shoes, Lorena rolled into the bed. As soon as her head touched the pillow, she was out. Lance had to wake her up for supper. His tough expression softened, as it always did when gazing at his new wife.

"Lorena, Darlin', you look pretty well washed out. Are you getting enough sleep these days?"

He gave her a long, comforting hug. She snuggled against his broad shoulder. He smelled like wood-smoke and cool fresh air. She pushed away long enough to blink up into his brown eyes. They were squinting, a sure sign he was worried about her. She sighed and took the opportunity to swing her long legs over the side of the mattress.

"Guess I must be worn out from that trip to Autreyville last night with Stuart. It was late when we got back."

She shrugged out of his embrace as she remembered. "And what were you doing yesterday afternoon when I tried to call you? I wanted Keith to make that drive down to the hospital for Harlan's body. Neither of you would answer your cell phones! Poor Stu had the willies all the way to Autreyville and back. I went with him to make sure he didn't scare himself into an accident on the road."

"Aw, Lorena, Darlin', we had to drive out into the woods to talk to the Kemper boys. No cell phone reception out there in the boonies, I guess."

Her anger did not soften. She hugged herself in high dragon mood. "So talking to a couple of kids was more important that helping me out?"

He patted her knee, the only thing available that wasn't stiffened against him at the moment.

"It was about Sister Susanna's death. Those kids gave us some good information, an important part of the puzzle of how that nun managed to drink high test shine."

"Oh," she said, and stared at her bare feet. She wiggled her toes, embarrassed by her tantrum.

"Sorry, Lance," she said and leaned into his warm bulk. "Don't know why I am so touchy these days! I don't like this new me. Not like the real me at all."

He lifted her long dark hair and kissed her behind the ear. It made her shiver, even coaxed a grin from her pouting lips.

"I'll take you any way you are, new you or old you. Every you seems OK with me. I love *every* you, don't you know?"

Belle's soft knock interrupted their fierce embrace.

"Supper time. John-Duncan's belly is growling. Zack and Mavis are waiting. Lilly-Belle is fussing. Better come while there's still food left on the table."

They broke apart, laughing, and hurried to the kitchen.

Chapter 41

Blanche

Blanche tapped her toe impatiently as she stood outside Lorena's embalming room. The clothing bag over her arm grew heavier as she waited for Lorena to answer her intercom. She had pressed the buzzer long and loud, but still no answer. Raysa touched her free hand to still the jangling of her bracelets.

"Blanche, give her time, for heaven's sake! Lorena is probably in the middle of embalming Harlan right now. Even the nimblest mortician needs time to take off her gloves and come to the door!"

Blanche did not favor being chastised. She gave Raysa a fierce glare and shook her head, setting her earrings to jangling a different tune than the noise of her bracelets.

"I did give her time to answer! This bag of clothing is heavy, don't you know? Makes my arm ache like fire just to keep it from falling to the floor." She thrust the bag at Raysa. "Here! You hold it and see how patient you can be!"

Lorena opened the door. She stared at her female kin and chuckled.

"Only you two would squabble over a bag of clothing." She shook her head, hiding a grin. "Here, give it to me. And thanks, both of you for bringing something decent for Harlan to wear. Right now he is only wearing a towel."

She stepped back and bowed the women into the embalming room.

Raysa walked right in, but Blanche hesitated just outside the door.

"Won't be anything disgusting to see, will there?" She fanned her face with her tiny purse.

Lorena's violet eyes were dark with sympathy, "Just the sad remains of an old man who couldn't live without his beloved wife, your sister, Bunny."

Blanche took tiny, tottering steps through the doorway. She stopped and stared at the body on the stainless steel table in the middle of the room.

"Ah, poor Harlan. He did carry on so when poor Bunny died."

"They were everything to each other," Raysa said and dabbed at her nose. She fished into her jacket pocket for a stick of cinnamon gum. As she unwrapped the foil and folded the pink gum into her mouth, she sighed.

"Don't you dare get all mushy on me now, Raysa!" Blanche snapped. "Harlan could be mean. Or don't you remember how rude he was to you when Mumma's Will was read?"

Raysa cracked her gum, an old habit that always brought comfort to her. She sighed again. "That's all in the past, Blanche. In the end, he was still just a lonely old man who lost his will to live."

Blanche finally turned her head to stare at her brother-in-law. Her bracelets tinkled softly as she reached out to touch his thin hair. "He did love our Bunny," she said. "Poor old man."

Lorena took the garment bag and opened it on a nearby table. She fished out a grey business suit, including matching vest, and a dark, patterned tie. White shirt, of course. No respectable business man wore anything except a white shirt here in the deep south. Black polished shoes and matching socks remained in the bottom of the bag. No underwear. She turned to the still squabbling sisters and stared them into silence.

"What?" Blanche said.

"No underwear," Lorena said.

Raysa snickered. Blanche felt the warmth of rising heat on her face. She flapped her hands, setting her bracelets to jingling again.

"Well, I couldn't think of everything," she said, scowling at Lorena. "You all are just lucky Bunny gave me a key to the house before she died. Told me then, 'take care of my Harlan after I go, Sister, dear.' I tried but the stubborn man wouldn't even answer my knock on his door. I was half afraid he might call the Sheriff on me if I used the key to go check up on him."

Blanche huffed and shook her head. Raysa patted her flailing hands into blessed silence.

"Yes, good thing you had the key, Blanche. Saved us from breaking a window to get in."

Lorena chimed in. "Don't get into a hissy fit over clothes for Harlan, Blanche. It really doesn't matter what he might be wearing for his Wake. He ordered a closed coffin, Morley told me."

"What?" Blanche sputtered. "Then why did you ask me to fetch his good suit and all the rest of the folderol if nobody will be able to admire how well dressed he looks in his coffin?"

Lorena folded her arms and stared at the thin corpse on the table behind them. "It's just that … well, Harlan was a proud man. I figured he might want to approach the pearly gates decently dressed. A male pride thing, don't you know?"

Raysa nodded. "I remember how Mumma clutched at her night gown at the moment of her death, as if she, too, wanted to be modestly clothed as she entered heaven."

Mollified, Blanche settled down. She stared at her tiny feet, the toes of her feet tapping away on the shiny white tile of the embalming room. She took a step toward the door.

"Guess I better go back and hunt down skivves for him."

Lorena touched her stiff shoulder. "Don't leave yet, Blanche. I have plenty of death-wear clothing here I can use for Harlan. Besides, I need a personal favor. Really could use some of your wonderful fashion sense right now."

Blanche turned, surprised and pleased. After all, she was the expert on fashion in these parts. Everyone said so, especially her steady customers who frequented her little shop, "Blanche's Boutique."

"What do you need, Lorena? If I have it in my shop, I'll fetch it right over."

Lorena blushed and stared down at her plastic apron. It barely covered the growing baby bump that seemed to protrude at an alarming pace as the days went by.

"Do you have anything that might fit me now?" She gestured toward the lump that now swelled above her navel.

Blanche stepped back to assess Lorena's figure. She nodded thoughtfully.

"Something fashionable, yet concealing, to wear in public?"

Lorena sighed with relief. "Exactly. I don't want to call attention to myself right now. Especially during Harlan's Wake. No smock tops, you know?"

Blanche smiled. "Indeed I do. I think I have a few dresses in the shop that would work for you, not only now but in later months."

"I usually wear pant-suits during Wakes."

"A dress might be better for now. You could wear those fancy high boots Harlan surprised you with on your wedding day. They are just the thing to wear under a long skirt. Make you look professional, yet feminine."

"Hmmm," Lorena said, cracking her knuckles absently. She must have realized she was indulging in the childhood habit she tried to avoid, because she slapped her fingers and blushed.

Blanche grinned. "How about it, Sis? A change might do you good, right now."

Lorena nodded slowly. "All right Blanche. Maybe changing my dress code might help my attitude, too. Been mighty touchy lately. Thanks, both of you."

Lorena reached forward and gave both sisters a grateful hug.

Blanche withdrew first, flapping her hands and making her bracelets chime their discordant melody. Raysa stepped back and gave a prolonged professional stare at Lorena's baby bump. She cracked her gum.

"Uh, Lorena? Doc Huey wants you to come in Monday for a checkup. What time would be good for you?"

Lorena's violet eyes grew wide, dark with sudden fear.

"Monday? My next checkup isn't due for two weeks. Does Huey think there might be something wrong?"

She hugged her unborn baby and grew so pale, both women eased her into the nearest chair. Blanche fanned her with her purse.

"Now Lorena, don't fuss yourself now," Blanche said. "The family needs you to buck up and carry us through this new ordeal."

Blanche shot Raysa a glance filled with daggers.

Raysa smiled and shrugged. She patted Lorena on her thin shoulder.

"No big deal, Lorena. You know how careful Huey is about his beloved women, especially pregnant ones? It's just a precaution, after the shock of Sister Susanna, plus another family funeral."

Lorena still appeared pale and shaky as she sat in the chair, staring at Harlan's cold body which still waited to be decently dressed.

Raysa knelt beside her and wrapped one arm about Lorena's trembling body. She stared up into her pale face.

"Want me to help you with Harlan?" she asked.

Blanche squawked. "Raysa! You want to touch a dead body?" She shuddered until her earrings tinkled.

Raysa glanced up at her sister, shivering like a spooked kid in her tiny, high-heeled shoes.

"Wouldn't be the first time I handled a dead person, Blanche. It's just the mortal shell of a man after his spirit escaped his tired old body."

Blanche fled the embalming room, head held high, her heels making a fast tippa-tap as she escaped the presence of a dead body and her puzzling kin.

"You two are crazy to do that kind of work."

Just before the door slammed on her escaping figure, she flung back reassuring words for Lorena.

"I'll come an hour before the Wake tomorrow afternoon and bring you something suitable to wear, OK Lorena?"

"Thank you, Blanche," both women chorused as the door slammed.

Blanche heard their muted laughter as she escaped down the long white hallway.

Chapter 42

Belle

True to her promise, at one o'clock, Blanche brought another garment bag bursting with clothing for Lorena's approval. Belle had just cleared the dinner table and shooed John-Duncan into the room reserved for his video movies. A new Disney type production, something about two sisters, with plenty of singing, would keep him entertained for a couple of hours. As Belle shut the door, she smiled at the sound of Johnny as he sang along to the now familiar tunes.

"Let it go!" his deep voice rumbled. "Just let it go!"

Belle frowned slightly as she caught sight of that Bouton woman, with her high and mighty ways, walking through the door at the top of the stairs. *Didn't even had the courtesy to knock, first,* Belle thought. But she pasted a smile on her face anyway. Kin is kin, she had been taught from little up.

Mavis, baby on her shoulder, stepped back as Blanche entered the room.

"May I help you, Mrs. Bouton?" she said, jiggling the baby to quiet her fussing.

"Just have something for Lorena," Blanche said, staring at the baby.

You'd think she never saw an infant before, Belle thought scornfully. But she stepped forward to take that heavy looking bag sagging in Blanche's arms. *Kin is kin.*

132

"Here, let me take that bag for you, Mrs. Bouton. It looks too heavy for a bitty little woman like you to carry."

Blanche released the garment bag to the housekeeper. She rubbed the sore muscles in her arm.

"Should have had Stuart carry this for me," she said. "But he went over to Harlan's this afternoon, searching for something Uncle Morley asked about in order to settle the Parnell estate. Men! Where are they when you really need them?"

"Right here, Ma'am," Lance said, appearing suddenly at her side.

Blanche jumped in fright. Belle hid a grin. *Now that Lance, he sure is a big hunk of man,* she thought and turned away. Mavis, still jiggling the fussy baby, followed her aunt into the kitchen. Dishes to do up. Baby needed her bath. A busy afternoon ahead. *Lance can take care of Mrs. High and Mighty,* Belle thought and couldn't resist sharing a chuckle with Mavis.

Standing in the foyer, now holding the bag of clothing in his big paws, Lance smiled down on Blanche.

"You need a man to help you, Blanche? Here I am, at your service." He motioned to the garment bag. "Where do you want me to put this? I assume you meant to give this to us?"

Blanche flushed. "Yes, well, Lorena asked me to bring her some clothing this afternoon. Where is she, by the way? She needs to try on some of the stuff before she makes up her mind."

"In the shower right now. "I'll just put this on our bed until she comes out. Want to go and watch her get dressed?" he said.

Belle, lingering in the kitchen doorway, a drying towel in her hand, grinned at the leering expression on Lance's face. She knew that it was Lance, not Blanche, who longed to watch Lorena get dressed. She grinned as Blanche blushed to the roots of her dyed blonde hair.

"No, no. Not necessary. I'll just wait out here until Lorena tries on the dresses." She stared around wildly until Lance took pity and pointed out the comfortable chairs in the living room, just off the kitchen.

"It won't be long before my gal gets out of the shower. Viewing hours start in an hour. She always wants everything to look just so hunky-dory before the doors open for the Wake. I'll go make sure she isn't too delayed," he said with a leer.

Blanche sat down with a long relieved sigh. Lance hurried down a hallway toward their bedroom. The garment bag rustled as he quick-stepped his way toward his wife. *Didn't want to miss any important flash of skin, I bet,* Belle thought, grinning as she turned back to her kitchen duties. *Randy old man,* she thought, but it made her chuckle as she finished up the kitchen chores.

Makes this old heart feel good to see young people so in love. What an inspiring example of a good marriage! Wish my husband had been a decent man like Lance. Made her a tad sad, comparing her marriage to the Lundrum's, but life can be like that. *You can't always get what you want,* she thought and gave herself a big shake to lighten her mood once again. Belle felt mighty blessed to be working for Lorena and Lance, she knew. *And that Johnny!* She loved him, for sure. As if he was her real son.

Chapter 43

The Wake

Lance and Lorena waited at the top of the stairway until Zack's chair-lift stopped at the bottom and their hired help transferred himself from the lift to his motorized wheelchair. Their maintenance man and valued companion to John-Duncan had changed out of his plaid work shirt and cut off jeans into his Marine uniform. Aunt Belle had carefully pressed the sleeves and pants into the required military pleats. Mavis helped by carefully tucking and pinning the pant legs underneath so they fit his shortened legs.

"Zack looks pretty snazzy all dressed up," Lance said, giving Lorena a hug as they started down the steps.

She smiled. "He told me he wanted to look 'professional today. Like a real doorman, not just a legless man in a wheelchair' as he opens the door for the mourners." Lorena smiled up at Lance. "Zack is such a treasure for our family. A blessing."

"You're looking pretty snazzy yourself this afternoon, Mrs. Lundrum," he said.

His gaze roamed over the beautiful dress Lorena wore. He admired the long skirted dress which hung down below her knees to mid-calf. Her dressy boots, a wedding gift from him specially made by Boot-Daddy, covered her bare legs. The gown's high waist allowed the black skirt to drape carefully over the newly formed curves in her lower abdomen without clinging to her altered figure. The upper part of the dress, in dark violet pleats, matched the exact color of Lorena's eyes.

Lorena patted the bodice, smoothing out invisible wrinkles. Her eyes narrowed with worry.

"Do you think this is too fancy for me to wear, Lance? I usually wear a dark jacket over matching slacks."

Lance gave her a warm hug that folded her into his broad chest.

" I think Blanche did herself proud, coming up with that pretty dress in such a short time. And you, my dear, look absolutely beautiful wearing it."

Zack grinned as he held open the door to the Viewing room. "You'll knock 'em dead, Lorena," he said. Then grinning at his unintended pun, he added. "Not that you need the business, of course."

All three laughed as they walked into the main Viewing room for Harlan's Wake. Lorena greeted Blanche, dressed in a beautiful, two piece silk suit of a subdued blue color designed to set off Blanche's bright blue eyes. Earrings tinkled as the two women embraced. Beside her, Raysa waited for her hug. Her pretty soft brown dress draped across her generous bosom and accented her deep brown eyes and hair. Her kiss on Lorena's cheek gave off a faint odor of cinnamon gum.

Lorena broke apart to check the floral arrangements and check that enough tissue boxes dotted the end tables. She straightened a few chairs, whisked invisible dust off every bare surface, then drew a long sigh.

"OK, Zack. Unlock the front door."

Lance gave her a quick kiss and hug, then left for his assignment: the roving security detail. His main job was to keep sticky fingered "mourners" from stuffing loot into their pockets or purses. Harlan had been a rich man who recently closed his mill and laid off hundreds of men and women. Rumors circulating in the area hinted of high jinks and revenge on the "Mean old man" responsible for the new poverty haunting their homes. Lance kept his eyes peeled at the mortuary.

Meanwhile, Keith stood guard at Harlan's mini-mansion, and would continue to do so even if he had to stay there all day and into the long night ahead. Saturdays sometimes brought out the crazies, tavern dwellers looking to create a bit of mayhem just for the general hell of it. Both lawmen knew how quickly boozy hi-jinks, fueled by too much alcohol and a tad of resentment, could turn from playful fun to something else entirely. Arson, or worse, the burning of crosses on the lawn of Harlan Parnell's fancy mansion. Lance would join him, if necessary, for the night watch.

That afternoon, Zack kept busy opening and closing the front door as mourners entered. Some left soon after, polite people paying their respect to the grieving family. Most stuck around, mainly the Old Guard, people from the previous generation where Wakes were one of the main attractions for gleaning and spreading juicy gossip. They lined the walls of the Viewing room, old women and men, leaning toward each other, hiding words behind their wrinkled hands. Too proud to wear their hearing aids, they were forced to whisper so loudly, all and sundry could overhear their conversations.

"A closed coffin! Can you believe it? Not normal to mourn the dearly departed unless you can actually see them laid out!"

"Scandalous! What was Lorena thinking? She didn't hide that poor Bunny after she died of cancer. Poor thing, so wasted away, I could barely recognize her. Yet she kept the lid open."

"What are they trying to hide, I wonder?"

"Maybe that fancy coffin is filled with money. Wouldn't put it past the old skinflint to try to take it with him."

Gray heads nodded wisely.

"He did love his almighty dollar."

"And wasn't too fond of sharing it, either!"

"Bet he couldn't buy his way into heaven, I do believe," someone said smugly.

Lorena had enough. She clapped her hands loudly to still the hateful chatter. When all eyes turned to her, she smiled grimly.

"For all of you people who might be wondering why the newly departed is in a closed coffin," she nodded toward Harlan's earthly remains, "I can tell you the why of it. If you might be interested in the truth?" Her fierce glare silenced every lingering murmur.

"Mr. Parnell stated quite clearly in his final Will that his body be in a *closed* coffin. He must have had good reasons for his orders, but as his mortician, it is not up to me to change or *question the why of it.* I am bound, by law, to follow his written and signed legal instructions, and I did."

She gestured toward the closed coffin, nodded curtly, and stalked out of the room.

Zack at the front door, grinned and applauded silently. Lance, entering the room, gave his wife the high sign and a big wink. The Old Guard gave a collective gasp, reared back against their chairs, glanced at each other and slowly climbed to their feet. Canes tapped as they headed toward the door. Zack gave each one a smile and a sincere, "Thank you for coming. The family appreciates your support."

Soon, only family members stood in the Viewing room. They stared at each other, their mouths hanging open in surprise at Lorena's outspoken speech. Raysa was the first one to snicker. She tried to hide it with a cough, but soon everyone began to laugh. Even Stuart's nose quit dripping for the moment. Blanche fanned herself with her purse.

"My, Lorena, you do like to stir up mischief, don't you?"

Raysa snickered again. "Good for you, Sis," she said, and patted her shoulder.

"They were just so hateful! All their mean-spirited talk about Harlan, as if he was the devil incarnate. I just couldn't take it any longer!"

Blanche gave in and laughed too. "You do realize, Lorena, that Harlan's Wake, and your thoughtful little speech, will keep those old gossips chattering for months, don't you know?

"Let those mean old biddies talk!" Lance said, crossing the room.

He hustled across the thick carpet and gave his wife a long hug.

"I did overhear some nice talk, though, Darlin'," he said, dropping a quick kiss on her cheek. "Seems the younger women just loved your dress. When they asked me about it, I told them, 'Blanche's Boutique'. Bet you have local women pounding down your door, come Monday, Blanche."

"Why thank you, Lance." Blanche blushed with pleasure.

Zack called from the foyer, "Is it time to lock up, Boss?"

Even before the family members checked their watches, Lorena nodded and waved to him. "Go ahead. This Wake is over. I don't think any more people will be coming. Harlan didn't have any family except us."

"And even fewer friends," Stuart said quietly, swiping his nose.

Lance gave Lorena another quick hug and kiss.

"I better go now, Darlin'. Keith will need extra help guarding the Parnell property. You might better booby-trap the coffin too, in case some greedy rednecks come back and decide to check out Harlan's coffin for a hidden stash of money."

Lorena grinned as she recalled an earlier time she had set a trap for a would be thief with mischief on his mind. She glanced at Harlan's coffin and sighed.

"Poor Harlan. How he howled that night. Sounded just like a werewolf."

She sighed again. "No need to worry about Harlan's coffin. He goes into the ground right now. Zack already dug the grave this morning."

"Need more help with that, Lorena?" Zack said. He flexed his arms. "I have pretty strong pecs, you know. Comes from all the therapy, learning to lift myself into my chair and such."

Lorena said, "Thanks! The high lift on the big tractor does most of the work, but I can always use the help of a strong man with good arms!"

Stuart hustled to help Lorena, too. Together they removed the decorative cloth that hid the gurney beneath and maneuvered the coffin through the Viewing room. Zack fetched the tractor from its shed and drove it close to the garage entrance. Lorena opened the big door, and with Stuart's help, pushed the gurney outside until the high lift hook was fastened onto a chain assembly around Harlan's coffin. The heavy metal coffin swayed a bit as Zack carefully drove over an open part of the cemetery to the waiting grave.

Lorena walked slowly beside the coffin, holding it steady. Raysa and Stuart followed behind. Blanche hung back. Stu glanced back at his wife, surprised to see her still standing in the garage opening. He beckoned to her with his hand. She shook her head.

"I can't stand to see someone put into the ground," she said and bit her lips.

"You sure?" he asked.

She nodded and turned away.

Lorena touched Stuart's hand. "Never mind, Stu. Plenty of people feel that way. Seeing the interment just makes the death too final for some people. Harlan is beyond caring, and his wife is waiting for him, anyhow."

Monsignor McGaffee, long black robes flapping in the slight breeze waited beside the open grave. As soon as the family gathered around the coffin, suspended by straps just above the open grave, the priest opened his small black bible. He drew a deep breath and addressed the surprised people staring at him.

"I know Mr. Parnell was not a member of our faith, nor any church that I know of, but he was still a son of God. Every person is beloved by our Almighty Father. No man should be buried without prayers said over him."

He glanced a silent question at Lorena. She nodded and folded her hands.

Monsignor read the traditional closing prayer for funerals. His voice neither hurried nor lingered over the familiar passages. Minutes later, he snapped the bible closed. He lifted his right hand and traced the Sign of the Cross over the coffin. Raysa and Lorena also blessed themselves with the ancient Sign, as did Zack waiting patiently on the tractor. Stuart swiped at his nose, trying not to call attention to himself, the only non-Catholic present.

"And may God have mercy on his soul," the priest said loudly.

"Amen!" the family echoed.

Monsignor nodded approval. He smiled sadly, turned and walked away, heading for the woods path that divided the Catholic cemetery from Lorena's general public burial ground. The little group of family stayed until Zack began back-filling the grave. Most swiped at tears as they turned and headed back to the house.

"It's always tough saying goodbye to family," Raysa said and sniffed.

"Even when an old grouch dies," Stuart said, swiping at his streaming nose.

"He was always kind to Bunny," Lorena said. But her heart felt heavy as she buried still another family member.

The sisters linked arms as they walked slowly through the cemetery. Blanche joined them as they approached the garage. Belle had fussed over a special supper to cheer up body and soul. As they neared the house, the delicious smells of a down home supper waiting, quickened their steps.

"I don't know about the rest of you, but I am starved," Lorena said.

Raysa chuckled. "Nothing like a death in the family to perk up a body's appetite."

She gave Lorena a warm hug. "Don't forget, Monday's appointment with Doc."

Lorena frowned slightly. "May have to change that, Raysa. Morley Wilton plans to read Harlan's will on Monday morning. Ten o'clock, he told me. And he wants all of us there, including Doc Huey."

"Wonder what the old reprobate put in his Will?" Blanche said, earrings tinkling.

Stuart shrugged. "Whatever it is, Morley is being mighty mysterious about it."

Chapter 44

Monsignor McGaffee

Sean McGaffee settled himself into his leather office chair. He wore a Stole draped around his neck over his usual dress blacks. Deacon Ned had asked for a private confession for some reason. Usually Seedy waited in line in the church during the scheduled penance services. These days, fewer and fewer of the faithful actually took advantage of the penance opportunities. Those who did, "Died in the wool" Catholics, preferred the privacy of the "black box" confessional. Even Deacon Ned used the black box, although Sean always recognized his voice anyway.

The office door opened and closed as Deacon Ned entered the room. *He looks scared to death,* the priest thought. He watched as Seedy dragged reluctant feet across the thick carpet toward the chair placed opposite him. They stared at each other across the wide desk. The pastor sighed and leaned back, waiting.

"Bless me Father, for I have sinned," Deacon Ned began.

His voice squeaked. Ned clutched his throat, visibly struggling to remain calm.

The priest leaned forward. Patience was not a virtue he possessed.

"For the love of God, Seedy, just spit it out. Whatever has you so terrified, remember that I represent Jesus, who is mercy incarnate. Whatever sin has you so tongue-tied that you are afraid to confess it, remember your training! God will understand, *and forgive you!*"

Deacon Ned closed his eyes. When he spoke, the words he mumbled came so fast, one word tumbling over the other, that Monsignor barely understood them.

"Father! Forgive me. I took money from the collections. Not for my own use, but for the Children's Saving Network. Those kids are so needy, and I just had to do something ... to help. Even the donations from the Rosary offerings wasn't enough to put a dent in the children's needs."

Deacon Ned's head hung down, eyes hidden from the astonished priest across the wide desk.

"How did you manage to pull off this *thievery* right under my nose?"

Seedy seemed to shrink from the thunder in his pastor's voice. Monsignor sighed and lowered his voice.

"I mean really, Seedy? How did you do it without anyone noticing or seeing you?"

"I hid a little bit of cash in the Rosary donation box, every weekend. Nobody caught on until Sister Susanna ..."

Sean's heart thumped in his chest. He hoped to God this confession was just about pilfering, not a prelude to an admission of murder. For the first time in years, Monsignor could not speak. It took a fervent, silent prayer for Ned's immortal soul before he could ask the question he dreaded to say aloud.

"Sister Susanna? What about Sister Susanna?"

"She found out, Monday, after daily Mass. I was on my way to fetch the money I hid, when I saw her stop at the rosary box and drop in a bunch of rosaries. I hid behind a pillar and watched as she took a second look into the box. She reached in and fished out the money. Sister looked around, but I don't think she saw me. It was dark in the church after you shut off the lights when Mass was over."

Ned paused to swipe tears from his cheeks.

"Father, I am so sorry. I knew stealing the money was wrong, but the children ..."

Sean crossed his arms across his chest to keep from reaching across the desk, grabbing up his foolish deacon, and giving him a good shaking. A long silence echoed in the quiet room. Monsignor closed his eyes and prayed. He waited. Finally the silence prodded Seedy into speech.

"And …"

The pastor's eyes flew open. "What? There's more?" Even Sean noticed the fear in his voice. "Tell me, Ned. Right now!"

"And I think I know who poisoned Sister Susanna!"

Monsignor collapsed into the comfort of his chair. His prayers had been answered. His foolish deacon had not committed murder, only petty larceny. He felt a deep shame at his quick relief. Ned's confession to him could remain hidden (not reported to the diocese). The sacred seal of the confessional meant the secret stayed between the two men. There would be no inquiry into his parish, no probing, uncomfortable questions about his leadership abilities. Then the deeper meaning of Seedy's revelation made him gasp. He leaned forward, his eyes probing Ned's face for any signs of deceit.

"You know who poisoned Sister?"

Ned burst into tears.

"Tell me, Deacon Ned, or consider your deacon status to be terminated."

Seedy sobbed into his hands for long moments. When he finally looked up, Sean saw a certain resolve in his deacon's swollen eyes.

"I hate to tell you this, Monsignor. Feels like I am a Judas to my own family. Please consider that the person is old and feeble. Maybe she has slipped into senility…"

Monsignor tapped his foot. "She?" His heart sank. He dreaded listening to another sordid tale of people he thought he knew, trusted, and certainly loved. "You said, 'she'?"

Ned's head hung low.

"She. Mema."

"Kat? My housekeeper? Your grandmother? I can't believe this."

Ned's eyes were pleading. "I'm not sure, but the more I thought about it, the more I suspect Mema. She never liked that nun, you know?"

Monsignor nodded. He had heard the women quarreling more than once as Sister Susanna worked on the parish ledger. *Some nuns can't help being abrasive, unfortunately,* he thought.

"So what makes you think Kat poisoned that nun?"

"Well, Father, a long story. You know Hannah, the housekeeper for Mayree and Royal Taylor?"

Monsignor nodded, mystified.

"Hannah brought me a bottle of Mountain Dew the other day. Only it wasn't a bottle of soda pop, it was the real thing. You know, what the moonshiners brew up in the woods?"

"Go on."

"Seems that the Kemper boys tried to pass it on to Petey Patterson, the paper boy. They told him it would cure what ails him."

Sean muttered a curse under his breath. "Did the boy get sick? I didn't hear anything about another poisoning."

"Hannah took it away from Petey. She came to visit me that afternoon. I took the bottle of shine and put in into the overflow refrigerator. You know, the one you keep in the lavatory next to the kitchen? You keep extra soda and beer there for company, you told me once. I put a rubber band around the neck and showed Mema so she wouldn't drink it."

Monsignor nodded. "So how did Sister's end up with it, then? And why would she even take it, let alone drink it? I never saw Susanna drink anything when she was here in the rectory. Not soda pop, nor coffee, nothing. Told me my water stank. Smelled like sulphur. Must be the well water."

Ned spread his hands. "I don't know what happened after that. And I'm afraid to ask my grandmother about it. It's just tearing me up, Monsignor. Did I cause the death of a holy nun by my carelessness?" He bent forward and sobbed into his lap.

Monsignor remained quiet for a long time as his deacon wept. Finally, he drew a long sigh and rapped on his desk to catch Ned's attention.

"Are you sorry for these sins and all your sins, Deacon Ned?"

"Yes, Father," Ned said and coughed.

"For your penance, I recommend you say a rosary a day for the rest of your life. *Plus!* Your sins will be forgiven *only* if you confront your grandmother about her role in the death of Sister Susanna."

"Oh, Monsignor! Please? I will do anything else to repent. Even walk a hundred miles on my knees, praying for forgiveness. But please don't make me ask Mema if she killed that nun!"

"It is a fitting penance, Deacon Ned. If you want forgiveness, you must obey. I have prayed about this. God requires it in order to forgive you for stealing from the church."

After Ned left to go into the church to pray, Sean felt a wave of shame engulf him. He realized the penance he doled out to his deacon was not a message from God, but resulted from his own uncertainty about how all of this would play out in the Bishop's office.

My housekeeper, a murderer? Thank God Ned's tearful revelation about the bottle of shine hidden in the refrigerator is covered under the Seal of Confession.

He knew if his superiors discovered the whole sordid mess, they might remove him from his position here and ship him off to some God-forsaken outpost in the rural bush.

His Excellency, the Bishop, might even demote me from Monsignor back to ordinary Father McGaffee!

Monsignor (for now) Sean McGaffee shuddered just contemplating that horrible thought.

Chapter 45

Saturday Evening Mass

Monsignor sighed heavily as he slipped the Chasuble over his head. The green garment, green because it was the prescribed color for Ordinary Time, fell into soft folds as it covered the white dress-like Alb beneath. He slid the small black audio transformer into a hidden pocket. The tiny microphone, wired to the transformer, clipped to the edge of his outer garment, the Chasuble.

The Sacristy was quiet. Altar Servers knew better than to chatter as their pastor prepared for Mass. Sean picked up a few notes he had hastily pulled together for this evening's homily.

Darned that Deacon, he thought.

It was Ned's turn to preach tonight. But after his exhausting confession, Ned insisted he felt unworthy to step foot on the Altar before he talked to his grandmother.

"It's my penance, Monsignor. You said so. I have to be right with Our Lord before I can serve Him on the sacred Altar."

Now I have to put together some meaningful thoughts to inspire the faithful parishioners waiting in the pews.

"Maybe something about Divine Mercy?" he muttered aloud.

Both Altar Servers jumped when he spoke. The young boy and girl stared at each other. Alex Paulson, shook a dark curl off his forehead and rolled his eyes. Mary Catherine Hewett played with her long blonde curls and stifled a giggle. The tightly coiled curls dangled down her back. She often played nervously with her hair during Mass. Pastor had warned her about it several times. He even suggested she put her elbows in restraints to curb her tendency to stroke her tangled curls. But both Servers were nervous now. They were not used to Monsignor talking to himself before Mass, or any other time for that matter. Sean glanced up, noticed the startled expressions on his acolytes, and grinned.

"Ready for Mass, guys?"

The Servers nodded. Mary Catherine picked up the tall crucifix. Alex carried the red book which held the Mass readings. They lined up and entered the Altar area. Monsignor grabbed the golden chain and rang the small bell attached to the doorway. The congregation in the pews stood up to welcome the beginning of Mass. Choirmaster spoke the name and page number of the Entrance hymn. Monsignor smiled as the church filled with the sound of people singing.

Mass went smoothly. The Homily, a bit short due to the rush of his preparations, also pleased the people in the pews. No one fell asleep this time. The pastor of St. Peter and Paul church relaxed into the ancient miracle of bread and wine changed into the actual Body and Blood of Christ. Most parishioners lined up to receive both the Host and the Sacred Blood from the cup.

It happened at the last Blessing. Monsignor had raised his right hand to bless the people before dismissing them, when a horrible shriek echoed through the building. An audible gasp froze the people in the pews. All turned around, straining to locate the origin of those anguished screams. Moments later, they turned back to the front as Deacon Ned raced across the Altar. He neither paused to genuflect in front of the Tabernacle, nor lowered his voice.

"Father! Father! Come now. Mema is having a heart attack. Help me, please? My grandmother is drying!"

Sean raced for the Sacred Oils, used for the Sacrament of the Sick. Before he disappeared into the Sacristy, he shouted to the people in the pews.

"Someone call 911!"

Even as both men raced through the rectory toward the upstairs living quarters of Kathleen Turnipseed, they heard a siren from the Oakhill volunteer fire department, summoning their trained EMT's.

Too late. By the time professional help arrived, Kathleen had breathed her last. The workers struggled to resuscitate the elderly woman to no avail. With Deacon Ned sobbing hysterically, they finally admitted defeat. The two men and a woman stepped away from the body. All turned to offer comfort to Ned.

"Sorry Deacon."

"We tried our best, Seedy, but I guess God wanted another angel," the soft-spoken woman said. She offered Ned a hug, but he pushed her away.

"My fault. All my fault. I shouldn't have asked her …"

Monsignor wrapped his long arms around Ned. One big hand covered Ned's mouth and silenced his babbling. He leaned down to hiss a command into his deacon's ear.

"Be quiet, Ned! Don't want to cause a scandal, do you?"

"But …?"

Seedy's protest sounded muffled behind the big hand covering his mouth. Later he would discover a smudge of Sacred Oil on his cheek, a remnant of the blessing ceremony Monsignor had performed on the dying old woman.

"We will talk about this later, Deacon Ned!"

Ned sobs continued. He fell across his grandmothers's body, weeping.

"I'm sorry. I am so sorry, Mema!"

The EMT's watched, their expressions sad. They too felt guilty for their failure to resuscitate the old woman.

Monsignor heaved a long sigh. "So what now, people?" he asked, staring at the three emergency workers. The men glanced at each other but said nothing. The woman spoke up.

"Our patient died outside a hospital setting. Someone needs to call the Coroner."

Chapter 46

Lorena and Lance

It was after supper at McGee's mortuary. Their company went home. Lorena and Lance relaxed in the living room. Zack and Mavis headed for their room, baby in arms. Lilly-Belle nodded sleepily on her father's shoulder as the wheelchair zoomed from the room.

The house phone rang.

"Now who could that be?" Lance grumbled as he rose to grab the nearest telephone. "Why can't people just leave us alone? Don't they realize we are in mourning?"

Keith had sent his boss home after the two men had sat too long in silence, watching Parnell's empty house.

"Go back to Lorena, Sheriff. I can handle any redneck that comes along. If they posse up in a mob, I will call you for help. Otherwise, I think Lorena needs you more than I do, right now. Go, get some rest. You look pretty worn out. Bet your new wife feels the same, don't ya think?"

Lance did feel worn out. He just didn't want to admit it to his new deputy. Didn't want that young whipper-snapper to think he couldn't do his professional duty, tired or not.

But the thought of Lorena, alone with her thoughts and regrets after the death of still another family member, worried hm. He didn't want his new wife to have any doubts about her decision to bring him into their extended family.

"She did look pretty worn out," he drawled. "Guess I better mosey on home and take care of her. She pushes herself too hard. Not good for her."

"Or for that baby of yours, either," Keith said, and smiled kindly.

Lance fired up his Harley and roared away.

Little good it did them to try to catch up on some rest, he thought now as he snatched up the telephone receiver.

"What?" Lance snapped.

"Oh, sorry, Monsignor."

He felt like biting off his tongue for being so rude to Lorena's friend and pastor.

"What? What's that you said? Old Mrs. Turnipseed died?"

Lance turned quickly as Lorena touched his elbow. When she reached for the phone, he gave it up gladly.

Lorena listened for a few moments, and nodded. "Thanks, Monsignor. We will be right over."

As she hung up, she turned to her husband, hovering at her elbow.

"Will you come, too, Lance? I might need help lifting the body."

"Sure, Darlin'. You know I would do anything to help you."

They took the hearse. Lance opened the driver's door. He struggled to fit his long legs beneath the steering wheel. Even with the seat all the way back, it felt as if his knees touched his chin as he crouched over the wheel.

"Lorena, Darlin', I know you are long legged, almost as tall as me, but this is a tight fit for this good old boy! Did you have this hearse special made for you? Custom made, I mean?"

She chuckled in the dimness of the vehicle. "No, Lance. Actually Duncan ordered it for me after I passed the State mortuary exams. Guess he never guessed I would marry a big hunk of man like you." She leaned across the console and gave his rough cheek a big smack.

Lance wriggled a bit, trying to settle his body deeper into the backrest. Finally, managing to feel a bit less constricted in the seat, he started the engine. When they arrived at the rectory of Saint Peter and Paul church, the EMT's met them at the door. The men carried the large bags of equipment. The woman told Lorena about what procedures they had preformed and their observations.

"It was pretty obvious the patient had already died by the time we got here," she said.

"We tried the usual restoring methods, the paddles, injections to restart her heart." She hung her head and swiped at a tear. "But Mrs. Turnipseed could not be saved. I'm sorry."

The men nodded and echoed her apology.

Lorena patted the woman's back. "Thanks for trying. I'm sure you did your best."

The EMT's nodded their thanks, turned and walked slowly through the dark parking lot.

Lorena, carrying a black body bag and Lance, following with the gurney, climbed the steps to Mrs. Turnipseed's bedroom. A chaotic scene met them at the upper doorway. Monsignor and Deacon Ned shouted at each other. Each man was red of face with clenched fists at their sides.

"Whoa!" Lance said and stepped between them. "What's going on here?" he bellowed over the shouts of the combatants.

They spoke together.

"Ned is just upset," Monsignor said loudly.

Even Lance noticed the fierce warning in the glare aimed at the deacon.

"He won't let me tell about Mema's mistake!"

Ned sniffed and swiped at his eyes with his sodden shirt sleeve.

Lorena stopped the quarrel with two softly spoken words.

"What mistake?"

The room fell silent. Monsignor and Ned, now held at arm's length by Lance's beefy hands, glared at each other. Both appeared reluctant to speak.

"What mistake?" Lance said. His voice, although low in tone, nevertheless commanded obedience.

Monsignor spoke first.

"Remember, *Deacon*, this is all covered by the Seal of the Confessional."

Monsignor backed away from the Sheriff's grip. He folded his arms and shot a haughty glance at Ned. Seedy was not cowed, not this time.

"Maybe you can't talk about my confession, but I can!" the deacon retorted.

Deacon Ned Turnipseed turned to face Lance and Lorena.

"I did it!" he blurted. "I killed her!"

He covered his face with his hands and wept.

Monsignor McGaffee snorted, lifted both hands above his head in a gesture of surrender, and stalked out of the bedroom

Chapter 47

Lorena

Lorena lightly touched the arm of Deacon Ned.

"Seedy, can you wait a few minutes before you tell us what happened?"

She nodded toward the corpse on the bed beneath the flowered quilt. His grandmother's body seemed to dwindle even as they watched.

"Let's take Mrs. Turnipseed out to the hearse. If we wait too long, her body might stiffen up and be too difficult to move down the steps."

Ned nodded and swiped at his eyes with his sleeve. His voice shook. "I can't stand to see her watching me." He stared at Mema's pale eyes, half open and empty of all expression.

"Yes, take her away."

Lorena reached across the corpse and gently closed both her eyes.

Despite his tears, Seedy did rise to the occasion and helped Lance and Lorena enclose his grandmother's body into the black body bag. He grabbed one end of the gurney and lifted the stretcher as he and Lance moved the gurney down the steps from garage apartment to the main hallway of the rectory. Lorena followed behind. When they reached the outside exit, they paused as Seedy opened the door. A handicapped ramp waited just outside. Lorena grabbed the end of the gurney and turned to the deacon.

"We can take it from here, Seedy. Why don't you wait inside. We will be right back. I'm sure Lance is very interested in what you have to say."

As the door closed behind them, Lance and Lorena maneuvered the gurney down the ramp and across the dark parking lot. The wheels made a clickety-clack across the rough surface beneath them. As Lorena opened the back doors of the hearse, Lance whirled to face the cemetery.

"Did you hear that, Darlin'?"

"Hear what?"

"Donno. Thought I heard something out in the cemetery."

Lorena's grin was hidden by darkness.

"Woolly-boogies after you, Lance?"

He shrugged and shook himself.

"Never did like a cemetery at night."

His deep chuckle sounded a mite bit forced to his wife.

"Better get used to it, Lance. We *live* surrounded by a cemetery."

He grunted and helped shove the gurney into the depths of the hearse. Lorena shut the wide back doors and grabbed his arm.

"Come on, my big brave hero. Let's go hear what Seedy has to say. Maybe we'll discover what happened to poor Sister Susanna."

"Finally!" Lance said, and quickened his steps through the threatening darkness.

Chapter 48

The Kemper Boys

Hiding behind the tallest headstone in the cemetery, the Kemper brothers waited and watched. When the door to the rectory slammed shut, they stalled a few minutes longer.

"Come on, Joey! I'm freezing!" Clyde said, his teeth chattering.

The boys had stayed out all night and all day Friday and Saturday, hiding in the cemetery to escape their father's promised whipping. They were tired, cold, and, most of all, ravenous. The boys raced across the parking lot and snatched at the front doors of the hearse. To their delight, neither front door was locked. They climbed in.

"Maybe they have some candy bars in here," Joey said. He rummaged around the console, feeling for the familiar shape of a Snickers or a Hershey bar. "Thank God!" he said, hastily unwrapping a candy bar and taking a huge bite. "I'm 'bout to fade away."

Clyde, in the driver's seat, found something even better.

"Lookie here, Joey! The fools left the keys!"

Joey rolled his eyes in the dimness of the dash lights. "Surely you're not thinking about stealing this car? Want the sheriff to come lookin' for us again?"

"Dumb old sheriff will never know. We can ditch the car somewhere in the woods. Let's just drive home, take Pa's belt strapping, and be done with it!" Clyde said.

Moments later the engine roared to life. Tires screeched as they raced for home.

"Nice and warm in here, Joey," Clyde said, snuggling his frozen backside into the soft leather seat.

Joey, still shivering from their long day hiding in the cemetery, reached to turn up the heater. A sound behind them stilled his hand.

"What was that?" Clyde said, turning to take a swat at his younger brother. "Quit fooling around, Joey! It was spooky enough hiding behind those old headstones. You trying to scare the wits out of me?"

Another frightening sound echoed through the hearse. Both boys turned their heads toward the corpse in the back. Zippered into the black body bag, the body of the newly deceased seemed to move.

Screech! Clyde stood on the brakes. Even before the hearse fully stopped, both boys yanked open their doors and fled, screaming like feline banshees with their tails afire. The hearse rolled to a stop in the middle of Rectory Lane.

Oscar Briarwood stood on the porch of his cabin, watching as the two boys raced away. Their screams and panicked flight made the old man grin and scratch his whiskers.

"Kemper boys! Something must have spooked them pretty good." He shaded his eyes from the glare of his porch light. He recognized the vehicle parked in the middle of the road. "McGee's hearse," he said and chuckled. "That'll teach those young'uns to stay out of trouble."

The old man was still chuckling as he went inside to call the Sheriff's office.

Chapter 49

The Confession

When Lorena and Lance entered the rectory, they found Monsignor and Deacon Ned waiting for them in the front office. Sean had removed his Mass vestments and washed his hands of the Sacred Oils. Ned had washed his face and seemed much calmer than before, now that his grandmother's body was not staring accusations at him from beyond the veil of death.

The Sheriff fished out the small notebook he always carried in his shirt pocket. He opened it, grabbed a pen from the desktop, and waited. Lorena did most of the questioning.

"Seedy, what did you mean when you said you killed her?"

"It was a mistake. I don't think Mema meant to hurt Sister Susanna."

"Your *grandmother* did something to that nun?"

Lance frowned. "But you said *you* killed her. What were you talking about, then?" he bellowed.

Ned shrank back into his chair. He stared at Monsignor, then bit his lips.

Lorena touched her husband's arm to quiet him. She knew Seedy would clam up completely if he felt threatened or afraid. She remembered him as a bullied schoolboy, hiding from the rough ways of the bigger, bolder kids in high school. She glanced at Monsignor. The priest's face look smug. *They must have talked to each other while we were outside,* she thought.

158

"Monsignor McGaffee," she said slowly. "I have to ask you to remove yourself from this room. The Sheriff needs to hear the *truth* from Deacon Ned, unfiltered by anyone, even you."

Sean stiffened. He drew himself up to his full height as he rose majestically from his office chair. "I am Ned's witness, nothing else," he said stiffly.

Lorena spoke softly. "Believe me, Father. We are not here to crucify your deacon. You can listen by the door, but please turn your back to the room. Every time Seedy even looks at you, his voice dries up."

Monsignor waited at the doorway, back turned to the room. Disapproval radiated from his folded arms and stiffened shoulders.

Lorena sighed. "Go on, Ned. Just tell us what happened. Nothing more. Nothing less."

Seedy heaved a long sigh. He dared not lift his eyes to stare at any of them in the room.

"Well, it began when Hannah brought me that bottle of Mountain Dew," he began.

Lorena noticed that Monsignor's posture sagged with relief as Seedy recited his tale.

"You mean, Hannah, the housekeeper for the Taylor's? Mayree and Royal? Amilee's parents?"

The Sheriff and Lorena, the Coroner, listened closely as Seedy explained about the doctored shine in an innocent-looking bottle of Mountain Dew. His story ended when he took the blame for showing his grandmother the green bottle with the rubber band around it.

"I swear, Lorena! I never thought Mema would use it to poison Sister Susanna."

"Those women never got along," Monsignor said, turning briefly toward the room.

Lance looked up from his notebook. "But you said *I killed her.* What did you mean? You still haven't explained that statement."

Ned glanced up, his eyes pleading for understanding. He stared at Monsignor's stiff back, turned once again away from the room.

"I talked to Father in confession about my worry that Mema might have somehow given that shine to the nun. Maybe just to make her sick? I know they fought a lot in the rectory. I could hear them shouting at each other from my office down the hall."

He gestured beyond the priest in the doorway. Barely visible in the darkened hallway, they noticed another door a few feet away.

"So you told Monsignor about your fears?" Lorena said, trying to get Seedy back to subject.

"Covered by the Seal of the Confessional!" Sean shouted without turning around.

Ned firmed up his quivering chin. "Father told me I had to talk to Mema about it!" He shot a defiant glare at Monsignor's stiffened back. "He told me if I wanted God for forgive me for my sins, I *had* to question my grandmother."

"So talking to Kat was your penance?"

Lorena wondered what terrible sins Seedy had confessed that might have merited such a strong penance. Wisely, she let that question fade from the conversation.

Ned stood up and shook his fist at Monsignor. "And that's when Mema had her heart attack! As soon as I started asking her questions about the moonshine bottle, she turned pale and started to cough and clutch at her chest. She fell over on the bed, groaning. I ran to the church to get Monsignor to help her."

Ned sank back into his chair and stared at the floor. His head drooped as his hands fell between his knees. He looked too exhausted to even place blame where it belonged, on the pastor who had forced him to question his beloved grandmother.

"But it was too late. Mema died," he murmured. "And it was all my fault!"

The silence in the room lasted long enough for each of them to squirm with discomfort.

Lance lowered his voice to a quiet rumble. "I hate to ask you this, Deacon Ned, but do you still have that bottle of doctored shine? Evidence, you know."

Ned shook his head. "I looked for it Tuesday, after we heard about Sister Susanna's death. Couldn't find it. Not anywhere in the garbage. I even searched the dumpster outside." He hung his head again. "That's when I started worrying about Mema, how she and that nun had quarreled the day before. I heard them yammering at each other from my office down the hall. I was afraid to ask Mema about it. Surely my grandmother couldn't deliberately kill someone?"

His frightened gaze skipped from person to person, desperately seeking reassurance.

Lance's cell phone rang. He tore his attention from Ned's face and dug deep into his pocket for the phone.

"Keith, what? *What?*"

Moments later Lance and Lorena hurried out the door. Both stopped at the top of the ramp and stared at the empty parking lot. No hearse waited for them.

Chapter 50

Lorena and Lance

Lance snorted. Hands on hips, his fierce gaze swept the empty parking lot of St. Peter and Paul Church.

"Keith was right. Those Kemper kids stole the hearse! Unbelievable!"

He snorted again, disgusted with himself.

"I can't believe it. I actually forgot to take the car keys with me."

Lorena smothered a giggle. She grabbed his elbow and gave it a squeeze. His expression, as he gazed down on her, resembled a sheep-dog caught in the act of demolishing a lamb. He shrugged and tried for a chuckle.

"It's only half a mile away, Darlin'. Are you up for a walk in the moonlight with a sorry ass sheriff?"

"Now, Lance. I sometimes forget and leave the keys in the ignition. I mean, who would have the guts to actually steal a hearse with a fresh body in the back?"

"I guess only the Kemper boys."

"Bet they got a big surprise if old Mrs. Turnipseed's body gave off that horrible croak behind them. It happens as the body cools off. The internal gas escapes and gives off what Duncan used to call The Death Rattle. I know it scared me many a time when I was a green kid, riding along after a death pickup."

She chucked and grabbed his arm.

"Bet that's why those Kemper boys abandoned the hearse. I can just see them, scared out of their wits," she grinned. "Serves them right, stealing my hearse with a fresh body in the back."

Lance tucked her arm under his as they began to walk down the middle of the road.

"Good thing those kids didn't get too far before they heard the death rattle. They came to a screeching halt and ran for the hills. Or so old Mr. Briarwood claimed. He's the one who called Keith about an abandoned hearse in the middle of the road."

He cleared his throat and patted his wife's hand.

"I am sorry, Darlin' for leaving the keys in the car. But I did hear something in the cemetery. You have to give me that."

"Yes, Dear," she said and giggled again.

They both sighed with relief as the examined the abandoned hearse.

"No damage, thank God," Lance said as he walked around the vehicle.

Lorena, after examining the body bag containing the newly deceased woman, backed out of the hearse and dusted off her hands.

"Nothing touched in the back, either," she said. "We were lucky, Lance," she said solemnly.

They climbed into the front seat in thoughtful silence. Lance started up the engine, then hesitated before sliding it into gear. He turned to Lorena.

"Are you going to press charges against the Kemper boys for stealing this?"

She hesitated, then shook her head. "I really don't want to bring theft charges against those boys. For one thing, it would be bad for business." She glanced toward the rear of the hearse. "If word got around about us 'losing' a body entrusted to me for a respectful funeral, it surely would not bode well with the Old Guard. I can hear those old biddies clacking about it already."

She shook her head and turned to him.

"Are you going to arrest those boys for theft, Sheriff?"

Lance drummed his thick fingers on the steering wheel.

"They did commit a felony, grand theft auto, but then they are both underage…"

"Can't we just overlook it this time? I mean those kids are just country boys," Lorena said.

Her fervent plea made him hesitate before he answered.

"Lorena, Darlin', I have to do something! Can't just shuck off a felony. I am the sheriff! Maybe Royal, the D.A. can work out something with a sympathetic judge…?"

His voice trailed away. Heavy silence filled the hearse as they both folded their arms in mutual disagreement. Finally, he snapped his thick fingers. The loud sound made her jump.

"I know! We can recommend a term of 'community service', instead of shipping them off to reform school. Do those overgrown kids good to pick up trash along the highway, instead of thinking about new ways to get into trouble."

"Sounds good to me," she said. "Picking up trash instead of them turning into trash. A fitting punishment for the Kemper boys."

She hesitated, then plunged on.

"What about Mrs. Turnipseed? Are you going to spread the news that this elderly woman likely killed Sister Susanna?" She waved a thumb toward the back of the hearse.

He sighed. "We have no real proof, Darlin'." He held up thick fingers to tick off his reasoning. "One, no confession, or at least none that would stand up in court. Seedy claimed his Mema never admitted anything, just clutched her heart and died in front of him."

"That's true," she said.

"Two, no murder weapon. No green bottle of doctored shine. Now if we found that green bottle we might have a clue of what really happened. Fingerprints, you know …" His voice trailed away with an echo of real regret. He shook himself and continued with his countdown.

"Three, no murderer to convict in court, now that Mrs. Turnipseed is surely dead."

He turned his head. "She is dead, right, Darlin'?"

"As a doornail, Lance. Let's go home and put our suspect in the cold room for the rest of the weekend. I can embalm her Monday evening."

Lorena put her head against the backrest and closed her eyes. Even before Lance put the vehicle in gear and it moved forward, she nodded off, exhausted.

Chapter 51

The Will

Early Monday morning, Raysa called Lorena. "I know Uncle Morley is coming at ten today, but Doc Huey wants you in the office this morning. Can you make it here by 8:30?"

Lorena yawned her answer. "If you insist! Might as well go in and get it over with. I swear Raysa, work keeps piling up on me. Now I have another dead person to embalm, plus plan the funeral." She yawned again.

"Sounds like your get up and go, got up and left. Happens during pregnancy, remember?"

Raysa's chuckle held a mild reproof.

"I was a lot younger when I carried John-Duncan. Younger and stronger."

Lorena scratched at the tangle of her long dark hair. "Need to shower, get dressed, and eat something. I am starved!" She rubbed her growing belly. "This baby sure makes me hungry all the time."

"See you at 8:30 then."

Raysa's laugh sounded smug to Lorena. She wondered about that as she yawned and headed to the bathroom, stumbling a bit as she dragged her sleepy self down the hallway.

* * *

At exactly ten a.m. sharp, Morley Wilton stood up. He moved to the fireplace in Parnell's main living room. He surveyed the crowded room. Stuart and Blanche sat together in the settee nearest the fireplace.

"Glad to see someone cleaned up this place," Stuart said and sniffed. Blanche nodded and fanned her face with her tiny purse. In the quiet room, her earrings tinkled.

Lance and Lorena snuggled in a larger couch opposite. Both of the newlyweds appeared stunned and a bit giddy. Doc Huey and Raysa sat in chairs lined up against the window wall. Raysa fished in her pocket and plucked out a stick of cinnamon gum. She offered half a stick to Doc, but he just smiled and shook his grizzled old head.

Sitting beside them, Mavis on a plain wooden chair, and Zack in his wheelchair, looked mystified at their requested presence here. Even more confused, Deacon Ned Turnipseed stared around the richly furnished room, his eyes mirroring his deep apprehension. None of the gathered family members, or those outside the family circle, cherished any delusions about receiving an inheritance. Harlan had been notoriously tight-fisted (some said downright mean!) about his money.

Morley set his briefcase on the mantle. He removed a fist full of paper fastened together with a large paperclip. The family lawyer turned to face the crowd.

"I know all of you are busy today, and every day, as we all are," he began.

Raysa cracked her gum. Stuart sniffed and dabbed at his nose. Blanche tapped her foot.

Doc spoke up. His words echoed what everyone seemed to be thinking. "Just skip the legal stuff, Morley. I have patients scheduled for later this morning. Can't keep them waiting while you make a Broadway production out of this."

Morley flushed. He placed a pair of horn-rimmed glasses on his face. He stared at them through the magnified lenses for long moments. Doc put his hands on the arms of his chair, a prelude to standing up and heading for the exit.

Morley cleared his throat loudly. "As I *started* to say, I intend to skip the usual humdrum legal stuff and just cut to the chase: the various people and causes Harlan Parnell deemed *worthy* to benefit from his considerable fortune."

Doc sat down. He dug out his ancient pocket watch and stared at it. With a meaningful glare at the lawyer, he snapped it shut and sighed. Raysa patted his hands, soothing him. Doc folded his arms.

From his perch in front of the fireplace, Morley paged through the legal document and began to read.

"To my wife's sister and brother-in-law, Stuart and Blanche Bouton I bequeath the sum of $500,000, to be held in trust with the accrued interest of such trust to be available every six months."

Morley stared over the top of his glasses as Blanche gave a great gasp.

"All that money!" she said. "I never expected …"

Stuart grinned. He had heard what his wife had missed, the important part of the gift, *to be held in trust.*

"Well, that will help keep us afloat from your spending binges, Blanche. A little cushion to keep the wolf from the door."

Blanche favored him with a hard glare. "Oh Stuart! You always look on the dark side. Besides, I don't spend that much really, don't you know?" Her earrings tinkled a denial of her outright lie.

Morley grinned and put his finger on his place in the document.

"There's more surprises, folks. Can I have your attention, please? Doc Huey has patients to see, remember?"

The crowd settled back into their seats. Morley grinned as he realized he had their full attention, *finally!* He flipped through another page of legal jargon, his lips moving as he scanned the document.

"Ah, here we go. 'To my wife's sister Raysa, I bequeath the sum of $500,000, to be held in trust until she sees fit to use this inheritance for a worthy cause.'"

Morley stared over the top of his glasses and cleared his throat. "This means, dear Raysa, that it is up to you to decide how to use Harlan's bequest. The dearly departed stressed that he trusted you to use the money wisely. Not on frivolity or such."

Morley glanced at Blanche and grinned. Blanche huffed, her eyes staring daggers, first at the lawyer, then at Raysa.

"How come you get to spend the money on whatever catches your eye, and I am stifled by Harlan's orders? Interest only, paid every six months! Why, that is a pittance! Birdseed to the starving. And you get to spend your money any time you want? Unfair!"

She aimed a hard glare at Morley. "Not fair at all, Morley!"

The lawyer smiled and shrugged. He spread his free hand in a gesture of helplessness.

"These are Harlan Parnell's last wishes. I am only the messenger."

Blanche sank back, tapping her foot and muttering. Her earrings tinkled their disapproval. Ignoring Blanche histrionics, the lawyer skimmed through the page before him.

"To Doc Huey, for his devotion to my wife, Bunny, and his careful treatment of her throughout her final illness, I bequeath my house and the acreage surrounding it. My dying wish is that Doc will transform this mansion into a treatment center for the victims of cancer. My fervent wish is that the new facility will be named in honor of my beloved wife, Bernice Wilton Parnell. My estate lawyer," Morley tapped his chest, "is charged with overseeing the remodeling of the house and grounds into a suitable place of welcome for all victims of cancer, and/or their families. All expenses occurred during this transformation from my private house into a public facility, shall be covered by a dedicated fund."

Morley glanced up. "What that means, Doc, is that no matter how much it costs, Mr. Parnell gave me the responsibility to pay for it out of a slush fund he established before his death. Nothing will come out of your own pocket."

Huey shook his head, completely bushwhacked by Harlan's generosity.

Raysa grabbed him and gave him a long hug. "Your dreams just came true, Doc. At last we can bring in oncology specialists to treat our cancer patients, instead of making them drive to Autreyville for their chemo or radiation!"

She turned to the lawyer, smiling. "Wish I could thank Harlan in person," she said, her brown eyes filling with tears. "He was a good man, in the end."

"And few people realized what a generous heart Harlan had until now," Doc said.

"Back to the Will," the lawyer said, clearing his throat of an unprofessional lump of emotion. He shook the now ragged clump of papers into a semblance of order.

"To Lorena McGee Lundrum, for her loving attention to my wife's body after cancer stole all her beauty, I bequeath the amount of $250,000, to be used for any future funerals of cancer victims. Lorena made my Bunny beautiful again after she died. My sincere hope is that other women, victims of that demon cancer, will also be made beautiful for their final public appearance. This sum may also be used to fund the funerals of cancer victims too poor to even afford a decent funeral. I trust that Lorena will use this inheritance wisely."

"What a thoughtful gift," Lorena said. Her violet eyes filled with tears.

Lance shook his head. "Harlan? Who could believe he cared so much? Most people thought him a mean-spirited soul. Now this."

He sank back in the softness of the lush couch and stared at his callused hands.

With a quick glance at Doc Huey, now glancing at his watch with a frown creasing his broad forehead, Morley continued.

"To Zachary Jakes, the groundskeeper at McGee's cemetery, for his careful and loving care of my wife's cemetery plot, I bequeath the sum of $250,000. My dying wish is that Zack uses this inheritance to further his education. In particular, my hope is that this fine young man, who gave so much in the fight for world peace, will decide to attend a collage of his choice, in whatever vocation he chooses."

Mavis burst into tears. Zack reached across the arm of his wheelchair to enfold his wife into a bear hug. "Finally, our dreams are coming true," he said, fighting back tears of gratitude.

Mavis climbed into his lap for a long kiss. When they broke apart, she swiped at her eyes and looked across the room. Lorena returned her glance, grinning from ear to ear. She did a silent clap motion with her hands.

"Miss Lorena, you don't know what this means to Zack and me. He wants to learn how to be a mortician, like you. He just admires you so much! Now we have the money for his education."

Lorena struggled out of the soft cushions of the couch. She hurried across the room, clutching her baby bump to keep it from upending her balance. Tottering, she almost fell into the wheelchair. Zack opened his arms. Lorena, Mavis and Zack thoroughly enjoyed a group hug.

Across the room, Lance's deep voice rumbled out his surprise. "Well, I'll be danged!" He turned to Morley. "This will certainly be a big help to Lorena. She is already worked off her feet. Now we can look forward to some much needed help somewhere down the line. Congratulations, Zack!"

"Yes, well, I did say there would be some surprises in the Will." Morley smirked. "There's one more bequest," he said.

The room grew quiet.

"To the man, Deacon Ned Turnipseed, locally known as Seedy, I bequeath the sum of $100,000, to be used however he sees fit in his role as Chairman of the Children's Saving Network. My beloved wife, Bunny, always loved children and asked me, on her deathbed, to help fund Seedy's special project for the 'Throw Away Children' of this area. She did so admire Ned's dedication to these under-privileged children."

Deacon Ned covered his face with shaky hands as he wept. "I don't deserve this," he said, over and over again. "I don't deserve this."

The room remained quiet as Morley finished up. He laid aside the papers and spoke directly to the room full of astonished people.

"Mr. Parnell not only remembered family members and certain special people in his Will, he also, with my help, sold his business, Parnell's Wood Mill. A new company from Mississippi, Woodwork-ers' United, will begin operations in a few weeks."

The lawyer folded up his paperwork and snapped shut his briefcase.

"That means that the local economy will receive a big boost in employment. People who previously worked at the Mill will be re-hired by the new company."

The lawyer jumped in surprise as the room erupted in applause. *First time I ever got a standing ovation,* Morley thought and hid a grin. Most survivors of the very rich left the proceedings with dark frowns of disappointed greed. He tapped Doc on the shoulder as he started out of the room.

"Go see your patients, Huey." Morley fished in his vest pocket. "Here's the key to this house. It's your's now, remember? And stick a smile on your face for a change."

Doc stood still and surprised the family lawyer with a big bear hug.

While they embraced, Blanche, followed by Stuart swiping at his nose, brushed past them. Blanche's tiny nose pointed skyward as she slung open the front door. Stuart glanced at Lorena, shrugged and spread his hands. "*See you tomorrow,*" he mouthed silently.

Lorena nodded and smiled. *Blanche could be snobby, all right,* she thought. But she felt a vast relief that Harlan had put Blanche's inheritance in trust. Otherwise, her friend and accountant, Stuart, might be driven to bankruptcy by his wife's irresponsible addiction to shopping.

Chapter 52

The News

Raysa called after Doc Huey. "Go along Doc, I'll be right behind you. Have to talk to Lorena for a bit."

Huey turned around and frowned. "Don't be too long, Princess. Mrs. Pennyweather is pretty sticky about having a woman in the exam room before she'll even let me listen to her heart, don't you know?"

Raysa nodded and grinned. She made a slight waving motion toward Huey, shooing him away. "By the time you change into your white coat, put new paper on the exam table, and open the office door, I'll be back to help you. Go along now."

He turned, grumbling, and shuffled toward the front foyer.

As Raysa watched his slumped figure, her eyes clouded with sadness.

"He's really slowing down these days," she said.

Lorena nodded. "I try not to think about it, but yes, Huey is really showing his age these past few weeks."

"That's what I want to talk to you two about," Raysa said.

She wiggled between Lorena and Lance as they sat on the wide couch. Like the walls of water in the Red Sea that Moses parted for the escaping slaves of Egypt, the couple moved right and left to accommodate Raysa's wide hips. Settling in for a brief discussion, Raysa drew a deep breath and plunged in.

"I think it's time I moved in with Doc. I spend most of my days and half my nights staying at his house, looking after him. Poor old

Rocket Man is left alone too often." She laughed a bit, then continued. "And you know what a dog left alone too often does: makes mischief. He keeps chasing squirrels through his doggy door and tearing up the house."

She heaved another long sigh.

"Would you two like to move into my house? That old Wilton mansion is just too big for a single woman like me. I would appreciate your family filling up the house, making it come alive again, if you know what I mean. Not just for Rocket Man's sake, you understand? Although he is included in the deal. John-Duncan should be able to keep the dog busy and happy. Hasn't he been begging for a dog, Lorena?"

Lorena nodded. "Yes indeed! John is desperate for a pet. I mean, video movies keep him entertained for a few hours, but a big guy like him needs his exercise too." She paused for a beat. "And of course, there will be a space problem later on."

Raysa reached across to pat Lorena's baby bump. All three grinned and nodded.

Lance rumbled, "Would ease the bedroom crunch. Getting a mite bit crowded at our house." He glanced toward Zack and Mavis, sitting in silence across the room. Lance smiled to soften any perceived complaint. "Not that Lorena and I don't love having you three living with us, but now ..."

Raysa glanced at Mavis and Zack. Their expressions mirrored astonishment and a cloudy flicker of fear.

Mavis said, "Does this mean we have to move?"

Lorena laughed. "Oh no, no! We want you all to live right where you are. After all, I'm going to need Zack's help in the embalming room later today. Old Mrs. Turnipseed died last night."

She glanced at Seedy, still slumped, weeping into his hands.

"So sorry about your grandmother, Ned."

Lorena sighed as she patted her baby bump, growing now at an alarming pace. Every day it blossomed bigger. She already felt like a blimp in her fifth month.

"In case you two haven't guessed," she said, "I'm expecting twins."

Even Seedy stilled his weeping to applaud the great news.

Raysa stood up. "Then we have a deal?"

Lance surprised his sis-in-law with a big hug. His whisper tickled her ear.

"You just solved one of my biggest worries," he said. "I didn't want our baby girl to live above the mortuary. Been afraid to even suggest it to my wife."

Lorena joined them for a group hug. "Guess we better start packing, Lance. And thank you so much for your generous heart, Raysa."

"Do we need to consult Uncle Morley about this?" Raysa said. "Mumma's Will gave me the house with the stipulation that I live there."

Lance shrugged. "Couldn't hurt. Don't want the family lawyer booting us out of the Wilton Mansion."

Raysa grinned. "We won't sign any sale papers or anything like that. On paper, I will still own the house, but you all can live there and settle in like true owners."

"That should take care of any objections from Morley," Lorena said. "We will just make the move and see what happens."

"Deal!"

While they laughed and hugged, Seedy stood and approached the happy group. He fished in his windbreaker pocket.

"Sheriff, could you do me a favor?" he asked. His eyes looked red and swollen.

"Depends on what you need, Son," Lance rumbled.

Deacon Ned extended a child's rosary toward the Sheriff. He drew a deep breath of courage.

"I believe this belonged to Amilee Taylor. I recognized it from when she made her First Communion. So pretty, a gift from her parents, if I remember correctly. I found it in the Rosary donation box at church."

He blanched at the memory of Sister Susanna's face as she plunked it into the donation box. Watching from the shadows, he wondered at the expression of smug satisfaction on the nun's face as she dropped it, and several other rosaries, into the box.

Then she found the money, he thought and grew even paler. Monsignor had warned his Deacon not to mention anything about the stolen money, not to anyone, not even the Sheriff. Especially not to anyone at the Diocese.

"Now that Mr. Parnell gave me that inheritance, I can buy lots of rosaries, bibles, and other much needed supplies for the children in my care." His voice faltered.

"Maybe her parents might like Amilee's rosary back?" he whispered.

Lorena opened her hand to accept the rosary. Her eyes reflected kindness and awe.

"Mayree will probably be delighted to have her daughter's rosary back, Seedy. Thank you so much for bringing it here today."

Deacon Ned gulped and turned toward the door. Moments later, his entire body slumped with sorrow and repressed grief, he quietly escaped the house.

Much later, Lorena wondered how Deacon Ned could have known he would receive a bequest from a near-stranger which allowed him the financial means to return a donated rosary.

Maybe Seedy just knew Mayree would want Amilee's rosary back again?

Lorena had heard rumors a few months before that Seedy and Mayree worked closely together for the Children's Saving Network. They even attended a workshop in Atlanta about it. Gossip at the time insisted that hanky panky went on during that out of town trip. All that changed when Aimlee died. She shrugged off all thoughts of common gossip. *From what Royal told me, Mayree will be so relieved to get her daughter's rosary back again. Might help heal her grief a tiny bit, just being able to hold her beloved child's rosary once again.*

"Let's go home, Lance. Plenty to keep us busy there. Not only preparing Mrs. Turnipseed for her final appearance here on earth, but all the rest. Packing, breaking the news to John-Duncan that his wish for a dog is now coming true. Most of all, easing him into the idea of a new house, with a new bedroom for him. He doesn't like changes, but maybe the prospect of having Rocket Man to play with every day might convince him that moving is a great idea."

She turned to Mavis and Zack.

"Come on, you two. Time to go home."

Chapter 53

Sister Susanna

Sister Susanna slammed shut the bathroom door at the rectory. Her head throbbed with pain. *Darned that Kat!* she fumed in silence. The nerve of a mere housekeeper branding a nun "just a volunteer." The very thought of the implied insult scalded Susanna's soul. And, it made her headache even worse! She dug into her oversized purse for her migraine pills and slapped the bottle on the edge of the sink. Her hand found Royal's flask and fished it out. Sister had been grateful when she found the flask on Mayree's dresser the day before. No telling how many times her younger sister had secretly resorted to alcohol to numb her grief. Susanna had walked into the adjoining bathroom, rinsed out the flask and filled it with tap water. She had contemplated replacing the flask on the dresser of Mayree's bedroom, then changed her mind. Ducking into the guest bedroom, she dropped into her own purse.

Now, in the rectory bathroom, Susanna shook several pain pills into her palm, tossed them into her mouth, and tipped up the flask. Ugh! The mere smell of sulfur water made her gag. She spat the pills back into her hand. Dumping the tainted water down the sink, she gazed around, searching for something to wash down the pills. A small refrigerator stood in the corner of the cramped room. Susanna remembered Sean showing her the drinks stored inside when she first came to work for him. He had waved his thick hand toward the rows of red cans of Coke and silver cans of beer.

"You need anything to drink, Sister, help yourself."

As she pried open the small door, she noticed another drink hidden behind some silver beer cans. Mountain Dew, a green bottle, with a rubber band around its neck. Hmm, she thought, must belong to Kat! Otherwise why would it be hidden and marked with a rubber band?

Susanna reached for the green bottle. She unscrewed the cap and poured the contents into her flask. The small amount of liquid that didn't fit into the flask, Sister dumped down the sink. Shaking the bottle, she had a moment of regret. Now what do I do with the empty bottle? she wondered. Her head pounded. The room spun as she stared around the small lavatory. Can't leave it here, Kat would find out and go belly-aching to Sean with her tale of woe.

A loud knock on the door made her jump. Guilt ramped up her head pain.

"Sister? You all right in there?"

The dreaded voice of the housekeeper increased the throbbing in Susanna's head.

"Pah!" *The nun dropped the empty bottle, along with the rubber band, into her cavernous purse.*

"Fine!" *she said, pushed past Kathleen and headed for the rectory door.*

Once in the privacy of her borrowed car, Susanna tossed back the handful of migraine pills, opened the flask and took a long drink. Ugh! Tastes terrible! She unwrapped a chocolate bar and took a bite. Even that didn't ease the foul taste in her mouth. She started up the car and roared away from the parking lot.

Sister Susanna, a Coke fan since little up, had never tasted Mountain Dew before. She swiped one hand across her mouth to soften the lingering bitter taste. She wondered, idly, how anyone could prefer such an unpleasant soft drink when Coke was available at any gas station or country store. Still parched, she took another long swig of the potent brew. In a rush to get home and rest her weary head, her foot pressed down on the gas pedal.

Suddenly, her vision darkened. A river of pain knifed through her stomach. She gave a cry of fear as the flask slipped from her hand. Susanna barely had time to open the driver's window and fling out the empty green bottle before everything went completely black.

She was dead before she even hit the tree.

Epilogue

Clyde and Joey Kemper, dressed in faded orange jumpsuits provided by the highway department, stumbled along Rectory Drive. They used the poles in their hands as walking sticks. The brothers stared at the ground, hunting garbage flung by local litterbugs.

"Who knew church people could so trashy?" Joey complained as he stabbed a fast-food wrapper with the nail on his stick and transferred the garbage into his black plastic sack.

Clyde nodded grimly. "At least the D.A. didn't send us to reform school. I heard from someone that the gangs in there love beating up on new prisoners."

Joey shuddered. He stabbed at a piece of green plastic hidden in the tall weeds.

"Lookie here, Clyde," he said, waving the item on the end of his pole.

"Isn't that the same bottle that got us in so much trouble before, Joey?"

The brothers stared at the battered plastic bottle.

"Get rid of it!" Both boys spoke at the same time.

Clyde hastily dug a shallow hole with the tip of his pole. Joey crushed the bottle until it was a quarter of its original size and dropped it in. They both stomped dirt and moss into the hole until nothing of the green plastic would ever be found.

"What are you boys up to?"

The burly man supervising the work crew shouted from his seat on the tailgate of the pickup truck. He had followed the crew all morning, The man spit out a wad of chew in disgust. He had never seen such a group of lazy kids in his life.

"Just killing a black snake!" Clyde shouted.

"Almost bit me," Joey said, improvising.

"Get back to work!"

Chuck, the supervisor, stared at them. He shook his fist. Hidden behind his wrap around sunglasses, his hazel eyes turned a deep green. *Lazy rednecks,* he thought. *Why, my boys back home could work circles around this bunch of do-nothing southerners, even before my kids turned twelve!* He spat again. It had not been easy finding a job down here. All the practical experience he had gained while working his fields up north, meant nothing down here. *Lucky this job turned up when it did,* he thought. Didn't pay much, but he could live out of his camper truck for now. He couldn't go home, not yet. *Not until I win back my wife. Not going home without her!*

"Get back to work you lazy rednecks!"

The Kemper boys shot a wary glance toward the man on the tailgate.

"Yes, sir!" they said and moved away from the buried bottle.

As the boys resumed their highway cleanup jobs that long afternoon, they often cast smug glances at each other. Clyde made a swiping motion with his hand. Joey nodded.

"Escaped a bullet that time," Joey whispered.

Clyde nodded. "Never again, brother. Never again."